REEDS AND MUD

BY THE SAME AUTHOR

E. P. DUTTON & COMPANY

REEDS AND MUD
"CAÑAS Y BARRO"

By VICENTE BLASCO IBAÑEZ

**Author of "The Four Horsemen of the Apocalypse,"
"Mare Nostrum," "Blood and Sand," "The Mob," etc.**

Translated from the Spanish by
ISAAC GOLDBERG

E. P. DUTTON & COMPANY : NEW YORK

REEDS AND MUD

REEDS AND MUD

I

AS on every afternoon, the mail-boat announced its arrival at Palmar with several bugle blasts.

The boatman, a wizened little fellow, with an amputated ear, went from door to door receiving orders for Valencia, and on arriving at the open spaces in the single street of the village he would blow the bugle anew to give notice of his presence to the cabins scattered along the banks of the canal. A cloud of almost naked urchins followed after the boatman with a certain admiration. They felt a deep respect for the man who crossed the lake of Albufera four times a day, carrying off to Valencia the best fish of the lake and bringing back a thousand things from a city that seemed mysterious and fantastic to these gamins brought up on an island of reeds and mud.

Out of Cañamèl's tavern, which was the leading establishment of Palmar, a group of reapers, sacks on their shoulders, sauntered in the direction of the boat, which was to take them back to their districts. The women thronged the banks of the canal, which resembled a street in Venice, its sides covered with huts and *viveros*[1] where the fishermen kept eels.

On the dead water, bright as tin, the mail-boat rested

---

[1] Thatch-covered pondlets where eels are kept alive.

motionless: it looked like a huge coffin laden with persons and packages, its gunwales almost on a level with the stream. The triangular sail, dotted with dark patches, was topped by colorless tatters which in other years had been a Spanish flag, informing of the official character of the old hulk.

An unbearable stench rose about the vessel. Its planks had become saturated with the odor of eel-baskets and the grime of hundreds of passengers: a nauseating mixture of gelatinous skins, scales of fish bred in the mud, dirty feet and filthy clothes, which by constant friction had smoothed and polished the seats of the boat.

The passengers, for the most part reapers who came from Perelló, the extreme end of Albufera, on the edge of the sea, were shouting at the top of their lungs for the boatman to set sail as soon as possible. The vessel was already full! There was no room for any more people! ...

This was so; but the little fellow, turning toward them the stump of his ear, which, it seemed, had been cut off so that he should not hear them, placed leisurely about the boat the baskets and the sacks that the women handed him from the shore. Each of these consignments provoked protests: the passengers were milling about or changing places, and those from Palmar who came aboard received with evangelical comment the outpouring of insults to which they were already accustomed. A little patience! As much room as they'd find in heaven! ...

The boat settled alarmingly on receiving so much cargo, but the boatman showed not the slightest concern, accustomed as he was to hazardous trips. There was not a foot of room left. Two men were standing on the gunwale, grasping the rigging to hold themselves up; another lay along the prow, like a ship's figurehead. Nevertheless the impassive boatman blew still another blast from his bugle amid general protest. . . . Christ! Didn't the old robber have enough yet? Were they going to spend the whole afternoon there, under the September sun, which scorched their sides and burnt their backs? . . . .

Suddenly a hush fell over the crowd and the people on board beheld approaching them, on the bank of the canal, a man supported by two women,—a white, shivering spectre with glittering eyes, wrapped in a woollen bedblanket. The waters seemed to boil with the heat of that summer afternoon; everybody on board was perspiring, doing his best to keep free of the sticky contact with his neighbor; yet this man was shivering, his teeth chattering from fever chills, as if the world had for him been plunged into eternal night. The women who were supporting him protested coarsely when they noticed that the people on the boat did not make way. They should make room for him: he was a sick man, a laborer. While reaping rice he had caught the cursed tertian fever of Albufera, and was on his way to Ruzafa to be cured in the home of some relatives. . . . Couldn't they act like Christians? For pity's sake! Move over!

And the quivering, fever-stricken spectre repeated the words like an echo, sobbing with his shudders:

"*Per caritat! per caritat!* . . . ."

He was pushed in, without any effort on the part of the self-satisfied crowd to make way, and not finding a place, sank down among the feet of the passengers, stretching himself out amid nauseating surroundings on the deck, his face thrust against filthy hempen sandals and mud-caked boots. The people seemed accustomed to such scenes. This boat served every purpose; it transported cargoes for meals, for the hospital, for the cemetery. Every day sick persons took passage, bound for the suburb of Ruzafa, where the denizens of Palmar, lacking facilities for treatment, hired lodgings for the cure of the tertian fever. When some wretched fellow without a boat of his own died, the coffin was placed under a seat of the mail-boat, and the vessel set sail with the same crowd of indifferent passengers, who laughed and conversed as usual, kicking the coffin, heedlessly.

After the sick man had disappeared from view, protest flamed up again. What was the earless fellow waiting for now? Was anybody missing? . . . . And then almost all the passengers greeted with guffaws a couple that came out through the door of Cañamèl's tavern, hard by the canal.

"It's Tío[1] Paco!" many of them shouted. "Tío Paco Cañamèl!"

The master of the inn, a massive, burly fellow bloated with dropsy, walked along with mincing steps. complaining like a child at every movement and leaning against his wife Neleta, a small woman with red, dishevelled hair, and warm greenish eyes that seemed to caress one with a velvety softness. Famous Cañamèl! Always sick and complaining, while his wife, who grew prettier and more amiable every day, reigned from behind her counter over all Palmar and Albufera. What he suffered from was the rich man's disease: too much money and too much high living. All you had to do was look at his paunch, his florid face, the cheeks that almost concealed his round little nose, and his eyes submerged in

---

[1] Tío: Uncle; colloquially an indefinite term of familiarity: old man.

billows of fat. If only they all might complain of the same illness! If he had to earn his living in water up to his waist, reaping rice, he wouldn't have time to think of being sick!

Cañamèl thrust one foot into the boat, painfully, with a weak groan, without letting go of Neleta, grumbling against the folk who made fun of his poor health. He knew how he felt! Ah, good Lord! And he took up his place in a corner which was vacated for him with that obsequious solicitude which countryfolk show to the rich, while his wife beside him openly received the blandishments of those who complimented her upon her beauty and her liveliness.

She helped her husband open a broad parasol, placed beside him a basket laden with provisions for a trip that would not last three hours, and then requested the boatman to take the very best care of her Paco. He was going to spend a short while in his cottage at Ruzafa. There he would receive the attention of the best physicians: the poor man was ill. She said these words smilingly, fondling the obese giant, who shook, at the first swaying of the boat, as if he were made of jelly. She paid no attention to the malicious ogling of the surrounding men, to the ironic, crafty glances that, after resting upon her, were fixed upon the tavern-keeper, who was doubled up in his seat under the parasol, breathing with grunts of pain.

The boatman thrust his long pole against the bank, and the boat began to glide along the canal, followed by the voice of Neleta, who, still smiling enigmatically, begged all her friends to take good care of her husband.

The hens scampered along the rubbish of the bank, following the boat. The flocks of ducks fluttered around the

prow, clouding the mirror of the canal, in which were reflected upside down the village cabins, the black boats tied
at the water-line to the thatched fish-ponds, decorated at
their peaks with wooden crosses, as if to place the eels inside under divine protection.

Issuing from the canal the mail-boat began to glide
along the rice-fields,—vast fields of liquid mud mottled
with bronze stalks. The reapers, immersed in the water,
advanced sickle in hand, and their tiny boats, black and
narrow as gondolas, received in their bottoms the sheaves
that were to be taken to the threshing floor. In the midst
of this aquatic vegetation, which seemed like a prolonga-
tion of the canals, there arose at intervals, above the little
islands of mud, white dwellings topped by chimneys.
These were the machines that flooded and drained the
fields, according to the needs of cultivation.

The high sloping banks concealed the maze of canals,
the wide, broad thoroughfares through which glided the
sail-boats laden with cargoes of rice. Their hulls remained
out of sight and their large triangular sails floated above
the green of the fields, in the silence of the afternoon, like
ghosts.

The passengers surveyed the fields like expert connois-
seurs, giving their opinions of the harvests and deploring
the bad luck of those whose holdings had been invaded
by nitre, which killed the rice.

The boat sailed along through tranquil canals, whose
water was of a yellowish color, with the golden glint of
tea. At the bottom, the aquatic plants bent their heads beneath the touch of the keel. The silence and the smooth-
ness of the water magnified all sounds. During the moments when there would be a lull in the conversation,

there could clearly be heard the painful respiration of the sick man stretched out beneath a bench, and the persistent groans of Cañamèl as he breathed, with his beard sunk in his chest. From the distant and almost invisible boats, came the sounds magnified by the calm, of a pole falling upon a deck, the creaking of a mast, the voices of the boatmen crying to one another so as to prevent a collision in the windings of the canals.

The earless pilot dropped his pole, and, jumping over the knees of the passengers, ran from one end of the vessel to the other, arranging the sail so as to take advantage of the slight afternoon breeze.

They had now entered the lake, in that part of the Albufera which is obstructed by sedge and islands, and where a nice care must be exercised in sailing. The horizon grew broader. On one side was the dark, wavy line of the pines of the Dehesa, which separates the Albufera from the sea, the almost virgin forest which extends for leagues and leagues, where wild bulls feed and large reptiles dwell in the dark, seen by few, but talked of with terror during night conversations. On the opposite side, the immense plain of the rice-fields merges into the horizon toward Sollana and Sueca, blending with the distant mountains. In the foreground, the sedge and the islets concealed the open lake, and among them the vessel made its way, mowing down the aquatic plants with its prow, its sail scraping against the reeds that leaned out from the shores. Meshes of tangled plants, gelatinous, like vicious tentacles, rose to the surface, twining about the boatman's pole; the eye could try in vain to plumb the bottom of this dark, foul-smelling vegetation, in the depths of which swarmed the creatures of the mud. All eyes expressed the same thought: whoever fell into those waters would find it hard to get out.

A herd of bulls was grazing on the beach of reeds and pools that bordered the Dehesa. Some of them had swum to the nearby islands, and, sunk in mire up to their bellies, were ruminating in the reed grass, splashing loudly about. They were huge, filthy beasts, with enormous horns and slavering snouts, their backs covered with scabs. They looked wildly at the laden vessel that was sailing by them, and as they shook their heads they scattered a cloud of mosquitos that soon returned to their curly manes.

At a short distance, on a bank that was little more than a neck of mud between two sheets of water, the passengers could make out a man hiding in a squatting posture. Those from Palmar recognized him.

"It's Sangonera!" they shouted. "Sangonera the drunkard!"

And waving their hats to him, they yelled and asked where he had begged his drink that morning, and whether he was considering spending the night there where he was. Sangonera did not move; but, weary of the laughter and the shouting of those on board, he at last stood up, and executing a graceful pirouette, slapped himself several times upon his back as a scornful gesture, then gravely squatted down again.

At the sight of him when he stood up the laughter redoubled, provoked by his strange appearance. His hat was decorated with a lofty plume of flowers from the Dehesa, and on his breast, and around his sash as well, were entwined some of the wild bell-flowers that grow among the reeds along the banks.

Everybody talked about him. Notorious Sangonera!

There wasn't his like in all the lake towns. He had firmly resolved never to work like the rest of mankind, asserting that labor was an insult to God, and he spent his days looking for someone to treat him to a drink. He would get drunk in Perelló and sleep it off in Palmar; he would guzzle in Palmar, to awake on the following day in Saler; and if there were festivities going on among the land folk, he would be found in Silla or Catarroja hunting up, among the people who cultivated fields in the Albufera, a generous soul to invite him to drink. It was a miracle that his corpse had not been found at the bottom of a canal, after so many trips on foot across the lake, dead drunk, following the boundaries of the rice-fields, which were as narrow as the edge of an ax, going through the sluice-gates with the water up to his breasts and walking over spots of sliding mud where nobody dared to venture without a boat. The Albufera was his home. His instinct as a child of the lake rescued him from danger, and many a night, as he entered Cañamèl's tavern to beg a glass, he was as viscous to the touch and smelled as much of the mire as an eel itself.

Catching the drift of the conversation, the tavern-keeper would murmur amidst his groans. Sangonera! A shameless good-for-nothing! He had chased the drunkard out of his house a thousand times! . . . . And the bystanders laughed as they recalled the vagabond's strange decorations, his mania for covering himself with flowers and weaving himself garlands like a savage as soon as the wine began to take effect in his famished stomach.

The vessel was penetrating into the lake. Between two masses of sedge resembling the jetties of a harbor, could be seen a large stretch of smooth, shining water of a whitish blue. This was the *lluent,* the real Albufera, the open lake, with its thickets of reeds stretching for long distances, wherein the birds of the lake, so ruthlessly pursued by the hunters from the city, fled for refuge. The boat coasted along the borders of the Dehesa, where certain muddy bogs covered with water were slowly being converted into rice fields.

In a little lagoon enclosed by banks of mud a man of powerful muscles was dumping basketfuls of dirt from his boat. The passengers gazed at him with admiration. This was Tío Tono, the son of Tío Paloma, and the father in turn of Tonet *el Cubano* (the Cuban). And as they named this last fellow many glanced slyly in Cañamèl's direction; the tavern-keeper continued to grumble as if he had heard nothing.

There was not in all Albufera a more industrious fellow than Tío Tono. He had taken it into his head to become a landed proprietor, to have his rice-fields and not have to live from fishing, like Tío Paloma, who was the oldest boatman in Albufera; and all alone—since his family lent him assistance only sporadically, growing weary of the vast extent of the enterprise—he was filling in with earth the deep lagoon that had been ceded to him by a wealthy woman who did not know what to do with it.

It was a matter of years, perhaps of an entire life-time, for a lone man. Tío Paloma poked fun at him; his son helped him now and then, only to declare that he was exhausted after a few days of it, and Tío Tono, with a faith that could not be shaken, went on with the work, aided only by La Borda, a poor little waif whom his late wife had taken out of the foundling hospital,—a creature who was exceedingly timid but as persevering in her work as he himself.

Greetings, Tío Tono, and don't give up! You'll be reaping rice from your field! And the boat sailed off without the obstinate laborer raising his head for more than a moment to reply to the ironic greetings.

A little farther on, in a tiny bark as small as a coffin, they caught sight of Tío Paloma near a row of stakes, placing his nets; he would draw them in on the following day.

On the mail-boat a discussion arose as to whether he were nearer ninety, or a hundred years old. What that man had seen, without ever leaving Albufera! The personages that he had dealt with! . . . . And they repeated the tales, which had been exaggerated by popular credulity, of his insolent familiarities with General Prim, whom he had served as boatman in that worthy's hunting trips over the lake; his rudeness to the great ladies, and even to queens. The old man, as if he had divined that he was the subject of these commentaries and was quite sated with fame, remained bent over, examining the nets, showing his back, covered with a large-checked blouse, and the black ragged cap jammed down upon his thin, large ears which seemed not to belong to his head at all. As the boat sailed past him he raised his head, revealing the dark chasm of his toothless mouth and the circles of reddish wrinkles that converged around his deep eyes, which were lively with glances of ironic brightness.

The wind began to rise. The sail swelled with new shocks and the heavily-laden vessel inclined so much that the shoulders of those who were seated at the gunwale were splashed. Around the prow the water, violently cut, rippled and gurgled more and more loudly. They were now in the real Albufera, in the immense *lluent*, blue and as smooth as a Venetian mirror, portraying upside down the vessels and the distant shores with their slightly serpentine outline. The clouds seemed to roll at the bottom of the lake like locks of white wool; on the beach of the Dehesa some hunters followed by dogs were mirrored in the stream, walking along with bowed heads. The large villages of the Ribera, their land concealed by the distance, seemed to float upon the lake.

The wind, growing gradually stronger, changed the surface of the Albufera. The undulations grew more noticeable, the waters took on a greenish hue, like that of the sea, the bottom of the lake was hidden and on the banks of thick sand formed from shells the waves began to throw yellowish locks of spume, soapy bubbles that shone iridescent in the sunlight.

The boat glided along the Dehesa and before it there passed rapidly the sandy hills, whose crests were topped by the guards' huts, the thick curtains of thickets, and the groups of twisted pines weird in shape like bundles of writhing limbs. The passengers, kindled by the velocity of the boat, excited by the danger to which they were exposed by the vessel's sailing with one of its sides on a level with the water, shouted greetings to the other barks that passed in the distance, and put out their hands to feel the impact of the waves lashed by their rapid progress. The water whirled around the helm. At a short distance swam two *capuzones*, dark birds that plunged into the water and after long immersion thrust out their heads again, amusing the passengers with these fishing maneuvers. Farther away, on the *matas,* the large islands of aquatic cane-plantations, the coots and the *collvèrts* rose in flight as the boat approached, but slowly, as if they felt that these were peaceful folk. Some of the passengers grew red with emotion as they beheld them. . . . What an excellent target! Why should the law prohibit anybody from shooting them without permission, just as he pleased? And while the more bellicose waxed indignant, there came from the bottom of the boat the groans of the sick man, while Cañamèl sobbed like a child, scorched by the rays of the setting sun that stole in under his hat.

The forest seemed to withdraw toward the sea, leaving between it and the Albufera a vast, flat plain, covered with wild vegetation and cleft here and there by the shining lamina of a tiny lagoon.

This was the plain of Sancha. A flock of goats tended by a boy was grazing in the underbrush, and at sight of it there rose in the memories of these children of Albufera the tradition which had given its name to the plain.

Those from the inland who were returning to their homes after having earned the big pay of the harvest asked who was this Sancha that the women named with such terror, and those of the lake told the stranger nearest to them the simple legend that they had all learned in their childhood.

A little goatherd like the one who was now walking along the bank was formerly tending his goats on the self-same plain. But that was many years ago,—many! . . . . So many, that none of the oldest inhabitants of Albufera had known the goatherd: not even Tío Paloma himself.

The boy dwelt like a savage in the solitude, and the

boatmen who went fishing in the lake would hear him on calm mornings crying from afar:

"Sancha! Sancha! . . . ."

Sancha was a small serpent, the only friend he had. The evil creature would answer to his cries, and the goatherd, milking his choicest goats, would offer her a bowl of milk. Afterwards, during the warm hours of the day, the boy would make himself a set of pipes from the reeds that he cut from the sedge, and would play gently upon them, with the reptile at his feet. The snake would draw erect part of her body and contract it as if she wished to dance to the rhythm of the sweet tones. At other times the goatherd would amuse himself by undoing Sancha's coils, stretching her out in a straight line upon the sand, delighted to behold with what a nervous impulse she would coil up again. When, tired of these games, he would take his flock to the other end of the plain, the serpent would follow him like a little dog, or, twining about his legs would reach almost to his neck, remaining there languidly and motionless, with her diamond-like eyes fixed upon those of the youth; the down of his face stood on end at the hissing from her triangular mouth.

The people of Albufera considered him a sorcerer, and more than one woman of those who stole wood in the Dehesa, on beholding him approaching with Sancha dangling from his neck, would make the sign of the cross as if the devil himself had appeared. Thus they all understood how the goatherd could sleep in the forest without fear of the great reptiles that swarmed in the thicket. Sancha, who must be the devil, protected him from all harm.

The serpent grew, and the goatherd had become a man, when the inhabitants of the Albufera lost track of him. It

was learned that he had become a soldier and had gone off
to fight in the Italian wars. No other flock ever came to
graze in the wild plain. The fishermen, on landing, did not
care to venture among the high reeds that covered the
pestiferous lagoons. Sancha, for lack of the milk that the
goatherd used to give her, was forced to pursue the in-
numerable rabbits of the Dehesa.

Eight or ten years passed by, and one day the inhabitants of Saler saw traveling along the road from Valencia,
leaning against a staff, and with a knapsack on his shoulder, a soldier,—a meagre, yellowish-complexioned grenadier, with black leggings that reached above his knees, a
white jacket and balloon trousers of red cloth, with a military cap mitre-shaped stuck on his carefully curled and
plaited hair. His flowing mustache did not prevent his being recognized. It was the goatherd, who had come back,
longing to see again the land of his childhood. Skirting
the lake he took the road to the forest and reached the
swampy plain where once upon a time he used to tend his
flock. Nobody. The dragon-flies fluttered their wings with
a soft buzzing above the tall reeds, and in the pools hidden
beneath the underbrush the frogs splashed about, frightened by the approach of the grenadier.

"*Sancha! Sancha!*" cried the former goatherd softly.

Absolute silence. There came to him the somnolent
chant of an invisible boatman who was fishing in the
middle of the lake.

"*Sancha! Sancha!*" he cried again, this time at the top
of his voice.

And after he had repeated his call many times, he
noticed a disturbance in the tall grass and heard the crackle
of bent reeds, as if a heavy body were crawling along.

Amid the cane there shone two eyes on a level with his own, and there advanced a flat head, moving a forked fang and uttering a sinister snort that fairly froze his blood and petrified him on the spot. It was Sancha, but a Sancha grown huge, arrogant, rising to the height of a man, dragging her tail among the thickets till it was lost to view, with a multi-colored skin and a body as thick as the trunk of a pine.

"Sancha!" exclaimed the soldier, recoiling with fright. "How you have grown! . . . . How big you are!"

And he tried to flee. But his old friend, after her first astonishment had passed, seemed to recognize him and wound herself around his shoulders, hugging him with a coil of her wrinkled skin, shaken by nervous tremors. The soldier struggled to get free.

"Let go, Sancha, let go! Don't hug me. You're too big for that sort of game."

Another coil wound tightly about his arms, gripping them like a vise. The reptile's mouth caressed him as in bygone days; her breath blew through his mustache, causing him an anguished shudder, and in the meantime the coils contracted, tightened about him, until the soldier, stifled, his bones cracking, fell to the ground, bound in the coil of variegated rings.

A few days later some fishermen came upon his corpse: a shapeless mass, with the bones broken and the flesh livid from Sancha's overpowering embrace.

The strangers on board laughed to hear the tale, while the women moved their feet with a certain restlessness, imagining that the creature stirring and groaning near their skirts was Sancha, hiding in the bottom of the boat.

They had reached the end of the lake. Once again the

vessel entered a labyrinth of canals, and in the distance, far off, above the immense rice-field, could be made out the houses of Saler, the little town of the Albufera which is nearest Valencia. Its harbor was filled with countless tiny craft and large boats that cut the horizon with their rough, unshaped masts, like pines with the bark peeled off.

The afternoon was drawing to a close. The vessel glided along less rapidly over the still waters of the canal. The shadow of the sail passed like a cloud over the rice-fields that were reddened by the setting sun, and on the sloping banks, against a background of orange hue, the silhouettes of the passengers stood out.

There was a continuous file of persons returning from their fields, standing in their tiny black craft, gunwales almost on a level with the water. These skiffs were the horses of Albufera. From early childhood, all who were born into this lake-dwelling tribe learned to manage them. They were indispensable for working in the fields, for visiting a neighbor's house, for earning one's living. Along the canal came a child, a woman, or an old man, plying the pole dexterously, digging it into the muddy bed so as to send the shoe that served them as a vessel gliding over the still waters.

In the small canals near by, other little boats, hidden behind the low banks, were gliding along; above the sedge one could see the boatmen, their bodies erect and rigid, propelling themselves along by quick jabs of their fists.

From time to time the passengers on the mail-boat noticed a wide gap in the banks, through which the waters of the canal scattered with neither noise nor agitation, slumbering beneath a layer of slimy, floating verdure. These openings were barred by the eel nets stretched from stakes. As the boat approached, huge rats bounded from the rice lands, disappearing into the mud of the canals.

Those who before had been filled with the hunter's enthusiasm at sight of the lake game, felt their passion rise anew on seeing the canal rats. What a fine shot! An excellent supper! . . . .

The inland folk spat with disgust, amid the laughter and the protests of Albuferan people. A delicious morsel! How could they venture an opinion if they had never tried it? The rats of the marshes fed only upon rice; they were a dish fit for a prince. All you had to do was see them by the dozens in the Sueca market, skinned, hanging by their tails over the butchers' blocks. The rich folk bought them; the aristocracy of the Ribera towns ate nothing else. And Cañamèl, as if he felt it incumbent upon him as a rich man to say something, stopped groaning long enough to make the grave assertion that he knew but two animals in all the world without a gall: the dove and the rat. That settled it.

The conversation grew livelier. The strangers' demonstration of disgust inflamed the Albufera folk. The physical degeneration of the lake people, the poverty of a people deprived of meat, knowing no other animals than those it saw running about through the Dehesa, living all its life condemned to feed upon eels and the fish that lived in the mud, was revealed in the form of bragging, with the visible desire of astonishing the strangers by boasting of the strength of their stomachs. The women enumerated the excellencies of the rat as an ingredient of the *paella;* many had eaten it without realizing it, amazed at the sweet taste of an unknown meat. Others recalled the dishes made of serpents, praising highly the round, white sweet slices, which tasted far better than eels, and the earless boatman broke the silence he had maintained during the entire voyage to recall a certain newly born kitten that he had eaten with some friends in Cañamèl's tavern, cooked by a certain sailor who, as a result of having sailed all around the globe, had golden hands for such dishes.

It began to grow dark. The fields held deep shadows. The canal took on the whiteness of tin in the tenuous light of dusk. At the bottom of the water the first stars shone, trembling with the passage of the boat.

They were near Saler. Above the roofs of the cabins rose, between two pilasters, the bell of the house of the *Demaná,* where huntsmen and boatmen assembled on the eve of the lot-drawing for fishing and hunting grounds. Near the house could be seen a large diligence, which was to convey the mail-boat's passengers to the city.

The breeze died down, the sail fell lifeless against the mast, and the fellow with the amputated ear grasped his pole, thrusting it against the embankment to move his vessel.

A small boat laden with earth passed by, bound for the lake. A girl was plying the pole industriously at the prow, and at the other end she was being helped by a young man with a broad-brimmed hat of finely woven straw.

Everybody knew them. They were the children of Tío Tòni, carrying earth for his field: La Borda, that tireless foundling who was worth more than a man, and Tonet *el Cubano,* Tío Paloma's grandson, the handsomest young man in all Albufera,—a chap who had seen the world and had plenty to tell.

"Good-bye, *Bigòt!*[1]" they shouted to him familiarly.

---

[1] Mustache.

They had given him this nickname because of the mustache that accented his strong swarthy face—a decoration little known in the Albufera, where all men shaved their faces clean. Others asked him with ironical astonishment since when had he taken to work.

The skiff sailed on without any indication from Tonet, who had cast a rapid glance at the passengers, that he had heard the gibes.

Many looked with a certain insolence at Cañamèl, permitting themselves the same brutal jests that they uttered in his tavern. . . . Look out, Tío Paco! You are going to Valencia, while Tonet will spend the night in Palmar! . . . .

The inn-keeper at first pretended not to hear, until, not being able to bear it any longer, he straightened up with a nervous start, a flash of anger gleaming in his eyes. But the flabby bulk of his body seemed to weigh upon his will, and he sank back into his seat as if overwhelmed by the effort, once again groaning painfully and murmuring between plaints:

"Liars! Filthy liars!"

II

TÍO PALOMA'S cabin was situated at one end of Palmar.

A great fire had divided the town, changing its aspect. Half Palmar had been devoured by the flames. The straw huts had been rapidly reduced to ashes, and their owners, desiring thereafter to live without fear of fire, built structures of brick upon the charred sites, many of them pawning their scanty belongings in order to transport the material, which proved very costly due to having to ferry it across the lake. The part of the village destroyed by the fire was soon covered with cottages, their fronts painted rose, green, or blue. The other section of Palmar retained its original character, the roofs of the cabins round at front and back, like boats placed upside down upon mud walls.

The cabins extended from the little church plaza to the far end of the town near the Dehesa, separated from one another through fear of a fire, as if scattered at random.

Tío Paloma's cabin was the oldest. His father had built it in the days when not a human being could be found in Albufera free from the tremors of fever. The thickets at that time reached to the walls of the cabins. The hens disappeared at the very door of the house, according to Tío Paloma, and when they next showed up they brought with them a brood of newly hatched chicks. In those days otters were still hunted in the canals and the population of the lake was so small that the fishermen scarcely knew what to do with the fish that filled their nets. Valencia, to them, was the end of the world, and the only one to come from there had been the marshal Suchet, who was created, by King José, Duke of la Albufera and lord of the lake and the forest with all their wealth.

Recollection of this personage was the furthest back that Tío Paloma's memory could go. The old man imagined he could still see him, with his dishevelled hair and his flowing side-whiskers, dressed in a red frock-coat and a round hat, surrounded by men in bright uniforms who loaded his muskets for him. The marshal had gone hunting in Tío Paloma's father's boat, and the little urchin, hidden at the prow, had gazed at him with admiration. Many a time he had laughed at the gibberish in which the marshal lamented the decline of the nation or commented upon the events of a war between Spaniards and the English, only scant details of which had penetrated to the lake region.

Once he had gone with his father to Valencia to present the Duke of la Albufera with a marsh eel, notable for its size, and Suchet, attired in his grand uniform with its dazzling gold trimming, surrounded by officers who seemed satellites of his splendor, had received them smilingly.

When Tío Paloma became a man and, upon his father's death found himself the owner of the cabin and of two boats, there was no longer a duke of la Albufera, but instead, Knights commander, who governed it in the name of the king their master; excellent city folk who never came to the lake, allowing the fishers to pillage the Dehesa and freely hunt the birds that were bred in the sedge.

Those were the good old days, and when Tío Paloma, at the gatherings in Cañamèl's tavern, recalled them in his broken old voice, the younger men quivered with enthusiasm. Men then fished and hunted at the same time, without fear of guards or fines. At nightfall they came home with dozens of rabbits caught with their ferrets in the Dehesa, and in addition to this, baskets of fish and strings of birds shot in the canebrakes. Everything belonged to the king, and the king was far away. The Albufera did not, at that time, as it now did, belong to the State (whoever that gentleman might be!) nor was the hunting privilege controlled by contractors and Dehesa the property of lessees, so that the poor folk could not discharge a shot or gather a faggot without a guard rising before them with his bandoleer across his chest and his carbine aimed at them.

Tío Paloma had maintained the pre-eminence of his father. He was the foremost boatman of the lake, and no personage ever came to Albufera that he didn't take him for a trip among the reed islets, pointing out the curiosities of land and water. He recalled Isabel II in her youth, filling the entire poop of the decorated boat with her wide skirts, her rounding, girlish breast trembling at every thrust of the boatman's pole. His hearers would laugh at the recollection of his trip over the lake with Empress Eugenia. She sat in the prow, a svelte figure, dressed like an Amazon, with her musket in constant readiness, bringing down the birds that skilful beaters by sticks and shouts put up in flocks from the canebrakes; and at the other end, Tío Paloma, sly and crafty, with his old gun between his legs, shooting the birds that escaped the grand dame and calling the *collvèrts* to her attention, in a fantastic Spanish: "Your Majesty . . . . look! There comes a *collovierde* from behind."

Everybody liked the old boatman. He was insolent with the rudeness of a son of the lake; but the cajolery that was wanting in his speech was expressed by his gun, a venerable weapon, so much repaired that it was hard to tell just how much of the original gun was left. Tío Paloma was a wonderful marksman. His fame expanded in the mouths of the region's tale-bearers, who went so far as to assert that he had brought down four coots with a single shot. Whenever he wanted to flatter a mediocre marksman he would take up his position behind him in the boat and shoot at the same time so that the shots would blend, and the huntsman, seeing the birds fall, would be filled with astonishment at his own skill, while the boatman would maliciously make faces behind his back.

His favorite recollection was that of General Prim. He had made the general's acquaintance on a stormy night while carrying him across the lake in his boat. Those were the days of misfortune. The guards were approaching; the general was disguised as a workingman and was fleeing from Valencia, after having made an unsuccessful attempt to rouse the garrison to mutiny. Tío Paloma took him as far as the sea, and when he next saw him, years later, he was the head of the government and the idol of the nation. Abandoning political life, he once escaped from Madrid for a hunt in the lake, and Tío Paloma, bold and exceedingly familiar with him as a result of the old adventure, scolded him as if he were a little boy whenever he missed a shot. For Tío Paloma there did not exist any human greatness: men were divided into good hunters and bad. Whenever the hero discharged without hitting his target the boatman would get so furious that he would even use the familiar pronoun in addressing him. "General . . . . inability! And was this the brave fellow who had accomplished such wonders yonder in Morocco? . . . Look, look and learn." And while the famous pupil laughed, the boatman would shoot off his gun almost without looking, and the coot would fall like a lump of lead into the water.

All these anecdotes endowed Tío Paloma with great prestige among the lake people. What that man might not have been had he simply cared to open his mouth and ask whatever he pleased of his fellow men! . . . . But he was always taciturn and sharp-tongued; he treated highborn personages as if they were tavern cronies; he made them laugh with his insolence when he was in bad humor, and with his twisted, bilingual phrases when he meant to be affable.

He was content with life, despite the fact that it was becoming more and more difficult, because of his advancing age. A boatman, always a boatman! He despised the persons who cultivated the rice-fields. They were *labradores*[1] and to him this word signified the greatest affront.

He was proud to be a man of the water, and many a time he would follow the windings of the canals rather than shorten the distance by cutting across the banks. He never set foot willingly upon any other soil than that of the Dehesa, to send a few shots at rabbits, making off at the approach of the guards. If it were left entirely to him, he would gladly eat and sleep in his boat, which was

---

[1] Farmers, "landlubbers."

to him what the shell is to an aquatic animal. The instincts of the primitive lacustrian races lived again in
the old man.

All he desired for complete happiness was to be rid
of a family, to live like a fish of the lake or a bird of
the sedge, making his nest today on an islet and tomorrow in a canebrake. But his father had insisted upon his
getting married. He did not like to see that cabin, his
own handiwork, forsaken; and the bohemian of the lakes
found himself compelled to dwell in the society of his
kind,—to sleep beneath a straw roof, to contribute his
share toward the maintenance of the curate and to obey
the petty magistrate of the island, always some shameless
wretch,—according to his words—who, in order to avoid
work sought the favor and protection of influential men
in the city.

He could hardly recall what his wife had looked like.
She had spent many years of her life at his side, without
having left in his memory any recollection other than her
skill at mending nets and the knack she had for kneading
the bread for the entire week every Thursday, taking it to
an oven with a round, white cupola, resembling an African
ant-hill, which was situated at one of the ends of the
island.

They had had many children,—many; but all except
one had died "opportunely." They were pale, sickly creatures, engendered with a view to having them contribute
to the support of the house, by parents who came together
only with a desire of transmitting heat to each other,
trembling as they did with the swamp fever. The children seemed to be born bearing in their blood the shudders of the tertian fever. Some had died of consumption,

weakened by the insubstantial diet of fresh-water fish; others had been drowned by falling into the canals near the house; and if one survived,—the youngest,—it was to clutch tenaciously at life, with a mad desire to survive, confronting the fevers and sucking from the flaccid breasts of his mother the scant substance of an everlastingly sick creature.

Tío Paloma considered these misfortunes logical and indispensable. Folks should praise the Lord, who remembers the poor. It was repulsive to behold how families multiplied in poverty; and without the mercy of the Lord, who from time to time made a gap in this pest of children, there wouldn't be enough food in the lake for all and they'd be forced to devour one another.

When Tío Paloma's wife died he, already an old man, found himself the father of a seven-year old boy. The boatman and his son Tono remained alone in the cabin. The boy was as clever and industrious as his mother. He cooked meals, repaired the cabin, and took lessons from the neighboring housewives so that his father should not feel the absence of a woman in the household. He did all this with a serious mien, as if the terrible struggle he had made to survive had left in him ineradicable traces of sadness.

His father strode along with an air of satisfaction when he walked toward the boat followed by the little fellow, who was almost hidden beneath a heap of nets. He grew up rapidly, becoming daily stronger, and Tío Paloma would swell with pride to see with what strength he drew the *mornells* out of the water or sent the boat gliding across the lake.

"He's the most manly man in all Albufera," he would

say to his friends. "His body is now taking revenge for the sickness he had when he was a little one."

The women of Palmar were no less ready to sing the praises of his sound habits. He didn't get mixed up in the wild pranks of the young loafers who congregated in the tavern, nor did he gamble with certain scoundrels who, as soon as the fishing was over, would stretch out on their bellies across the reeds, behind some cabin, and spend hours shuffling a filthy deck of cards.

Always reserved and ready for work, Tono never occasioned his father the slightest displeasure. Tío Paloma, who could not fish in the company of others, since at the merest oversight he would grow furious and attack his companion, never scolded his son, and when, in a moment of ill humor he would issue an order to the boy, he would find that the child, having divined his intention, had already tackled the work.

When Tono grew to manhood, his father, fond of a nomadic existence and rebelling against all family ties, experienced the same desires that had been felt by the original Tío Paloma. What were these two men doing, isolated in the solitude of the old cabin? It was unpleasant for him to behold his son,—a broad, sinewy giant,—bending over the fireplace, in the center of the cabin, poking the fire and preparing the meal. Many a time he had felt remorse, contemplating his short, hairy hands, with their iron fingers, scrubbing pans and scraping the lake fish, removing with a knife the hard scales shining with metallic reflections.

During the winter nights they were like a couple of shipwrecked sailors who had taken refuge upon a desert island. Not a word between them, not a laugh, not a sound of a woman's voice to cheer them. The cabin was a gloomy place. In the center, the fire burned in a hearth on the floor,—a small square space enclosed by bricks. Opposite, the kitchen bench, with its row of poor pots and old bottles. On each side the partitions of the two rooms, made of reeds and mud, like the rest of the hut; and above the partition walls, which were only the height of a man, the interior of the black roofing, with a coat of soot, smoked from the fires of many years, with no air passage other than an opening in the straw covering, through which the stormy winds of winter entered with their shrill blasts. From the ceiling hung the waterproof garments of father and son, worn in the night fishing expeditions: stiff, heavy trousers, jackets—with a stick thrust from sleeve to sleeve—of coarse texture, yellow and shiny from the oil rubbings. The wind, entering through the gap that served as chimney, would sway these strange scarecrows, which caught in reflections on their oily surface the red light from the fireplace. It looked as if the two inhabitants of the cabin had hanged themselves from the ceiling.

Tío Paloma was bored. He liked to talk: in the tavern he could swear as much as he pleased, he maltreated the other fishermen, and dazzled them with his recollections of noted personages he had known; in his own house, however, he was at a loss for speech, and his words, eliciting no response from his silent and obedient son, were swallowed into a respectful and overpowering silence. The boatman said so himself, in the tavern, with his jovial, brutal manner. That son of his was a mighty fine chap, but he didn't take after his father at all; he was always so quiet and submissive. His late wife must have played some sort of trick on him.

One day he accosted Tono with the imperious expression of a father of the Latin type who allows his children no will of their own and disposes of their future and their lives without even troubling to consult them. He must marry: he wasn't at all well off like this; the house needed a woman. And Tono received this command as if he had been told to get the large boat ready for the following day to meet a hunter from Valencia at Saler. Very well. He would try to fulfil his father's order as soon as possible.

And while the youth looked about on his own account, the old boatman communicated his intentions to all the mothers of Palmar. His Tono wished to get married. Everything he owned would go to the boy: the cabin, the large boat with its new sail, and another old one which was even better; two smaller boats, and he could not recall how many nets, and on top of this, the virtues of the boy himself,—a hard worker, sober, with no vices and exempt from military service because he had drawn a lucky number. In short: he wasn't a wonderful match, but his Tono wasn't as poor as a toad in the canals. And besides, the sort of girls that there were in Palmar! . . . .

The old fellow, with his scorn of womankind, spat upon beholding the maidens from among whom his future daughter-in-law was to be chosen. No. These virgins of the lake weren't much to look at with their clothes that were washed in the filthy water of the canals, smelling of mud, and hands saturated with a viscous substance that seemed to penetrate to their very bones. Their hair discolored by the sun, whitish and scant, was scarcely enough to shade their thin, reddish faces, in which the eyes shone with the glow of a fever that was ever renewed by drinking from the waters of the lake. Their angular profiles, the slippery meagerness of their bodies, and the nauseating odor from their skirts, imparted to them a certain resemblance to the eel, as if a monotonous and unvaried diet of many generations had resulted in stamping upon these people the traits of the creature that served them as sustenance.

Tono chose one of these,—any one at all—the one who interposed the fewest obstacles to his shyness. The wedding took place and the old man had another person in the cabin to speak with and to scold. He felt a certain intense pleasure on seeing that his words did not fall into a vacuum and that his daughter-in-law raised her voice in protest against his ill-humored exactions.

Together with this source of satisfaction came a disappointment. His son appeared to have forgotten the family traditions. He scorned the lake, and went off to seek his living in the fields, and in September, when the rice was harvested and wages were high, he abandoned his boat and became a reaper, like many another who roused Tío Paloma's indignation. This labor of working in the mud, of scarring the fields, was all well enough for strangers, for those who dwelt far from Albufera. The children of the lake should be free of such slavery. Not for nothing had God placed them near that water, which was a blessing. In its depths was their food, and it was an absurdity, a disgrace, to work all day in mud up to your waist, your legs gnawed by leeches and your back scorched by the sun, just to reap a few ears that weren't

your own. Was his son going to become a *labrador?*
. . . . And as he asked this question the old man invested
his words with all the stupefaction, all the unbounded
amazement aroused by an unheard-of atrocity, as if someone had just told him that one fine day the whole lake of
Albufera would dry up.

Tono, for the first time in his life, dared to oppose his
father's wishes. He would fish, as usual, during the rest
of the year. But now he was married, the needs of the
house were greater, and it would be imprudent to scorn
the excellent wages of the harvest. He was paid more
than the others, because of his strength and his applica-
tion to the work. Times should be taken as they come;
rice was being more and more cultivated on the shores
of the lake, the old pools were being filled in with earth,
the poor were becoming rich, and he wasn't such a fool
that he was going to lose his share in the new life.

The boatman grumblingly accepted this transformation
in the customs of his house. The common-sense and the
seriousness of his son compelled a certain respect, but as
he leaned against his oar on the banks of the canal, con-
versing with other boatmen of the good old days, he protested vehemently. They were going to transform the Albufera! Within a few years nobody would know the
place. In the direction of Sueca they were installing iron
machinery in houses with huge chimneys and . . . . the
smoke rose from them in clouds! The old *norias,* so
peaceful and agreeable, with their wheels of decayed wood
and their black buckets, were to be replaced with infernal
machines that churned the waters with the noise of a
thousand devils. It would be a miracle if all the fish
didn't take to the sea, disgusted by such innovations!

They were going to cultivate everywhere; they were shovelling dirt and more dirt into the lake. As few years as yet remained to him, he would live to see the last eel, having no room in which to move, wriggle her tail in the direction of the mouth of the Perelló and disappear into the sea. And Tono mixed up in this piratical work! To think that a son of his, a Paloma, should have become a *labrador!* . . . . And the old man laughed as if he had imagined an utter impossibility.

Time passed and his daughter-in-law presented him with a grandson, Tonet, whom the grandfather on many an afternoon carried in his arms to the banks of the canal, twisting his pipe to one side of his toothless mouth so that the smoke should not trouble the little fellow. A devil of a kid, and how fetching he was! That ugly, lanky creature of a daughter-in-law was like all the other women of his family: they gave birth to offspring that didn't resemble their parents at all. The grandfather, fondling the little boy, thought of the future. He showed him to the comrades of his youth, who were becoming scarcer and scarcer with time, and prophesied the days to come.

"This little fellow will be one of us: his only house will be the boat. Before he's cut all his teeth he'll know how to handle an oar."

But before the infant cut his teeth, Tío Paloma met with the most unexpected event in all his life. He was told at the tavern that Tono had rented certain rice lands near Saler, the property of a woman in Valencia; and when that night he confronted his son, he was amazed to see that the man did not deny the crime.

When had anybody ever seen a Paloma with a master? The family had always lived free, as every son of God

must live who has any self-respect, seeking their sustenance in the air or in the water, hunting and fishing. His
masters had been the king and that blunt warrior who was
a Captain General in Valencia; masters who dwelt far off,
who did not oppress, and who could be tolerated because
of their greatness. But a son of his, renting land from
one of those idle, stylish city women, and every year
bringing her in cash a part of his labor! What an idea!
He was ready to go to talk to that woman and undo the
contract! The Palomas would serve nobody as long as
there was anything left to eat in the lake: even if it was
only frogs.

But the old man's surprise grew greater than ever before Tono's unexpected show of resistance. He had
thought the matter over well and was not disposed to re-
treat. He was thinking of his wife, of that little boy
whom she carried in her arms, and it filled him with ambition. Who were they? Lake beggars, living like savages in the cabin, with no other food than the creatures
of the canals, and compelled to flee like criminals before
the guards whenever they shot a bird to put in the pot.
Nothing but parasites of the hunters, eating meat only
when the strangers allowed them to take a share of their
provisions. And this poverty continued from fathers
to sons, as if they were to live forever moored to the mud
of the Albufera, with no more life or ambition than that
of a toad, which thinks itself happy in the reeds because
its finds insects on the surface of the water.

No; he was rebelling, he wished to lift the family out
of its wretched prostration; to work not only for the purpose of getting enough to eat, but to lay something aside.
The advantages of rice cultivation must be appreciated:

little work and great profit. It was a veritable blessing from heaven: nothing in the world offered more. You plant in June and harvest in September; a little fertilizer and a little work,—in all, three months: you reap the harvest, then the waters of the lake, swollen by the winter rains, cover the fields and, then, all done until the next year! You save what you earn, and during the rest of the months you fish in the sunlight and hunt on the sly to keep your family provided for. What more could be desired? . . . . His grandfather had been a poor man, and after a dog's life had accomplished only the building of this cabin, where they all dwelt in everlasting smoke. His father, whom he respected so much, had not been able to lay aside even a crumb for his old age. Let them permit him to work as he saw fit, and his son, his little Tonet, would be a rich man, he would cultivate fields whose vast extent would be lost to the view, and upon the site of the cabin perhaps in time there would arise the finest house in all Palmar. His father was wrong to get angry because his descendants cultivated the earth. It was better to be a farmer than to lead a wandering life about the lake, often suffering hunger and exposing oneself to a bullet from one of the guards of the Dehesa.

Tío Paloma, white with rage at his son's talk, stared fixedly at a pole lying close to the wall, and his hands moved toward it as if to seize it and crack his son's head with a stout blow. Had such a rebellion occurred in earlier days he surely would have broken his son's head for it, for in his old-fashioned conception of a father's authority he considered that he had the right to do so.

But he looked at his daughter-in-law with his grandson in her arms, and these two beings seemed to increase his son's stature, bringing him up to his own level. He was a father, one of his equals. For the first time he realized that Tono was no longer the boy who had made supper in the olden days, lowering his head in terror at a single glance. And quivering with rage because he could not strike him as he used to when he committed some error in the boat, he vented his protest in loud snorts. Very well: everybody to his own taste; the one to the lake and the other to his labor of flattening the soil. They would live together, since there was no other way out of it. His years did not permit him to sleep out on the middle of the lake, for he had got rheumatism in his old age; but aside from this, it would be as if they did not know each other. Ay, if the original Paloma,—the boatman of Suchet,—could lift his head and see the family disgrace! . . . .

The first year was one of unending torment for the old man. Entering the cabin at night he would encounter farming implements side by side with fishing apparatus. One day he stumbled across a plow that Tono had brought from the land to repair during the evening, and it produced upon him the effect of a monstrous dragon stretched out in the center of the cabin. All these blades of iron made him shiver with rage. It was enough merely to see a sickle lying a few paces away from one of his nets, for him to imagine directly that the curved blade would rise of its own volition and cut all his property; he would scold his daughter-in-law for her carelessness, ordering her at the top of his lungs to keep those *farmer's* implements away—way away from his own. On all sides were objects that suggested the cultivation of the land. And this, in the Paloma's cabin, where no steel had been known other than that of the knives used to clean fish! . . . .

Good Lord, it was enough to make a man burst with rage!

During the sowing season, when the lands were dry enough to plow, Tono would come home perspiring, after driving the hired horses all day long. His father would walk around him, sniffing with malignant delight, and afterwards would dash to the tavern, where his comrades of the good old days would be dozing, glass in hand. Gentlemen, a great piece of news! . . . . His son smelled horsy. Hee, hee! A horse on the island of Palmar! Now the world had truly gone topsy-turvy.

Apart from these outbursts, Tío Paloma maintained a cold, aloof attitude amid his son's family. He would come in at night with his *monòt* on his arm, a basket made of net and wooden hoops, containing some eels, and would shove his daughter-in-law aside with his foot, to make room for himself before the hearth. He prepared his own supper. Sometimes he would roll the eels around a stick and make them *al ast* (on the spit) broiling them on all sides patiently over the flames. At others he would hunt up his old pot in the boat, containing reserve provisions, and would cook *en such* an enormous tench, or fastidiously make a *sebollá,* mixing onions with eels, and using such large quantities that it seemed as though he were preparing a meal for the entire town.

The voracity of this old, wizened fellow was that of all of Albufera's old sons. He ate his heavy meal at night, when he returned to the cabin; seated on the floor, in a corner, with his pot between his knees, he would spend hours at a time, in silence, moving his old goat-like mouth from side to side, swallowing enormous quantities of food,—so much that it seemed impossible for the human stomach to contain it.

He ate his own food,—that which he had captured during the day,—and paid no attention to what his son's family ate, offering them nothing from his pot. Let everyone fatten upon his own labors! His eyes would glitter with malicious satisfaction when he would see upon the family table, as their only food, a pan of rice, while he picked the bones of some bird that he had shot in the sedge while the guards were far away.

Tono let his father do as he liked. Using compulsion on the old man was not to be thought of, so the isolation between him and the family continued. Little Tonet was the sole bond of union. Many times the grandson would approach Tío Paloma, as if attracted by the savory odor of his pot.

"*Tin, pobret, tin*," the old man would say, compassionately, as if he beheld the child in the greatest misery. "Take this, my poor child. Here."

And he would present him with a succulent, meaty thigh of a coot, smiling to see how the tot devoured it.

Whenever he cooked some *all y pebre* (fish stew) with his boon companions at the tavern, he would take along his grandson without saying a word to the parents.

At other times there would be a bigger feast. On a morning Tío Paloma, feeling the itch for adventure, would have embarked with some companion as old as himself for the thickets of the Dehesa. A long wait, stretched out upon their bellies, spying upon the guards, who were unaware of their presence. As soon as the rabbits appeared leaping through the stalks of the underbrush, fire!—two of them in the bag, and run for the boat, afterwards laughing, from the middle of the lake, at the guards dashing about here and there along the shore hunting in vain for the poachers. These bold stunts rejuvenated Tío Paloma. It was a treat to hear him, at night, while the game was being eaten in the tavern by comrades who had paid for the wine with which to wash it down, boasting about his great exploit. Not a youth of the present day was able to do as much! And when the more prudent spoke to him of the law and its penalties, the boatman's chest swelled proudly, though it was sunken with the years and the constant poling. The guards were nothing but tramps, who took that sort of a job because they didn't care to do real work; and the men who leased the hunting were a band of robbers, who wanted everything for themselves. . . . The Albufera belonged to him and to all the rest of the fisher-folk. If they had been born in a palace, they would have been monarchs. If the Lord had caused them to be born there, it was for some purpose. All the rest was a heap of lies invented by men.

And after devouring his supper, when there was scarcely any wine left in the jugs, Tío Paloma would contemplate his grandson asleep on his knees, and would show him to his friends. This little fellow would some day grow into a real son of the Albufera. His grandfather would see to his education, so he wouldn't follow in the evil footsteps of his father. He would use the musket with astounding skill, he would know the bed of the lake like an eel, and when his grandfather should die, all who came to hunt would find in the boat another Paloma, but one in the strength of youth, such as he himself was in the days when even the queen came to sit down in his boat, laughing at his jokes.

Apart from these moments of tenderness, the boatman continued his smoldering animosity against his son. He did not care to see the cursed lands that he cultivated, but he had them ever present in his mind's eye, and would laugh with diabolic joy on learning that Tono's affairs were going badly. The first year his fields were spoiled by nitre, just when the rice was beginning to mature, and the harvest came near being lost. Tío Paloma repeated the story of this misfortune to everybody, with the greatest delight; but when he noted how sad the family was, and saw how they had to skimp because of the large expenditures that had gone to waste, he felt a certain compassion and even broke the silence to counsel his son. Had he not yet been convinced that he was a man of the water, and not a farmer? He should leave the fields to the inland folk, who were of old used to tilling them. He was the son of a fisherman, and must return to the nets.

Tono, however, replied with ill-humored grunts, indicating his determination to go ahead, and the old man subsided into his silent hatred. Ah, the obstinate fellow! . . . . From then on, he called down all sorts of calamities upon his son's lands, as a means of conquering his proud resistance. He made no inquiries at home, but as his little skiff passed the large vessels coming from the direction of Saler, he would inquire as to the progress of the harvest and would feel a certain satisfaction when he was told that it would be a bad year. His obstinate son would die of hunger. He would even have to come to him on his knees and beg for the key to the old eel-pond with the roof of broken straw that he had near Palmar.

The storms at the end of summer filled him with delight. He longed to have the cataracts of heaven burst open; to have that stream of Torrente that poured into the lake of Albufera, supplying it with water, overflow the place from shore to shore; to have the lake, as sometimes occurred, flood over and submerge the ears that were ripe for harvest. The farmers would die of hunger; but there would be plenty of fish in the lake just the same, and he would have the satisfaction of beholding his son starving, begging his aid.

Fortunately for Tono, the wishes of the malevolent old fisherman were not fulfilled. The years immediately following were favorable; a certain comfort reigned in the cabin, and the ardent toiler foresaw, almost in the light of a happiness impossible of realization, a time when he might be tilling lands that were his own, and which would not carry with them the obligation to surrender to another almost the entire product.

A shadow clouded the family life. Tonet was growing up and his mother was sad. The boy would go to the lake with his grandfather; after, when he was older, he would accompany his father to the fields, and the poor woman would have to spend the day all alone in the cabin.

She was thinking of the future, and the coming loneliness filled her with fear. Ah, if she only had other children! . . . . It was a daughter for which she prayed so fervently to God. But the daughter did not come; she could not come, according to Tío Paloma. His daughter-in-law was unwell; women's trouble. She had been delivered of her child by women neighbors of Palmar, leaving her in such a condition, according to the old man, that she could never bear again. This was why she always seemed so ill, as white as paper, unable to be on her feet for very long at a time, and on some days dragging her-self along, with groans that she swallowed with her tears so as not to bother the men.

Tono was eager to fulfill his wife's desires. He had no objections to a girl in the house; she could help the sick woman. And together they made a trip to the city, bringing back with them a little girl of six years,—a timid, wild, ugly creature whom they had taken from the orphan asylum. Her name was Visanteta; but every-body, so that she should not forget her origin, and with that unconscious cruelty of coarse, unrefined spirits, called her La Borda.

The boatman grumbled with indignation. Another mouth to feed! . . . . Little Tonet, who was now ten, found this little girl quite to his taste, inflicting upon her all his whims and exactions of a pampered, only son.

La Borda found in the cabin no other affection than that of the sickly woman, who grew daily weaker and more wracked with pain. The unhappy woman deluded herself into believing that she had a daughter, and in the afternoon, seating the girl in the doorway of the cabin, face to the sun, she would comb her red hair, well anointed with oil.

The girl was like a frisky, obedient puppy that en-livened the cabin with its scampering here and there, resigned to all fatigue, submissive to all of Tonet's mis-chievous pranks. With a supreme effort of her arms she would drag along a pitcher as tall as herself, filled with water from the Dehesa, from the canal to the house. She would run all over the town at all hours on errands for her new mother, and at table she ate with lowered eyes, not daring to raise her spoon until the rest were half-way through the meal. Tío Paloma, with his silence and his ferocious glances, terrified her. At night, as the two rooms were occupied respectively by husband and wife, and by Tonet and his grandfather, she would sleep beside the hearth, in the middle of the cabin, upon the mud that oozed through the canvas that served as her bed, covering herself with the nets to keep off the draughts that blew down the chimney and through the cracked door gnawed full of holes by rats.

Her only pleasant hours came during those afternoons when all was calm and the men were either on the lake or in the fields; then she would sit down with her mother to sew sails or weave nets before the cabin door. The two conversed with the neighbors, amid the deep silence of the solitary, crooked grass-covered street, over which the hens strutted and the ducks waddled, cackling and flapping their damp white wings in the sunlight.

Tonet no longer attended the town school,—a damp cottage supported by the city council, where boys and girls, in an ill-smelling gathering, spent the day whining the alphabet or chanting prayers.

He was every inch a man, as his grandfather said, when he felt his muscles to see how hard they were and thumped the child's chest with his fist. At his age Tío Paloma had already been able to live on what he had himself caught, and had shot at every species of bird that flies in the Albufera.

The boy gladly followed his grandfather on his expeditions over land and water. He learned how to handle the pole and sped like lightning in one of Tío Paloma's little boats; when hunters came from Valencia, he would crouch in the prow of the boat and help his grandfather manage the sail, leaping to the bank at difficult moments to grasp the rope and drag the vessel in tow.

Then came the development of his skill in hunting. His grandfather's musket, a veritable arquebuse, which was easily to be distinguished from all other guns in Albufera by its report, he learned to handle with relative facility. Tío Paloma loaded heavily, and the first shots made the boy stagger; he all but fell head over heels into the bottom of the boat. Little by little he tamed the old beast and soon was bringing down coots, to the great delight of his grandfather.

That was the kind of education boys should receive. If the old man had his way, Tonet would eat nothing that he had not shot or fished with his own hands.

But after a year of training Tonet in this rude fashion, Tío Paloma noted a great slackening of interest on the part of his pupil. Tonet was fond of discharging shots and liked fishing. What he did not seem to be so fond of was getting up before daybreak and spending all day long with his arms stretched out moving the pole and pulling like a horse at the rope.

The boatman saw clearly that what his grandson detested, with instinctive repulsion that awoke his most spirited resistance, was work. In vain Tío Paloma spoke to him of the great fishing they'd do the following day at *el Recatì, el Rincón de la olla,* or some other point of Albufera. No sooner did the boatman turn his head than his grandson had disappeared. He preferred to scamper over the Dehesa with the good-for-nothings of the neighborhood, to stretch himself out beneath a pine and spend the hours listening to the chirping of the sparrows in the tufted crests or watching the white butterflies and the bronze bumble-bees flit about in the wild flowers.

The grandfather threatened, but to no avail. He tried to spank the boy, but Tonet, like a wild animal, would escape from him and look on the ground for rocks with which to defend himself. The old fellow became resigned to making his trips on the lake alone, as before.

He had spent his whole life working; his son Tono, although led astray by his agricultural enthusiasm, was stronger even than he for hard tasks. Then whom could that little terror have taken after? Lord! Where had he come from, with his endurance that was proof against all fatigue, with his fondness for lying about idle, basking for hours in the sun like a toad on the canal bank? . . . .

Everything in that world beyond which the old man had never set foot was undergoing a transformation. The Albufera was being entirely altered by the men with their cultivating, and families were being disfigured, as if the traditions of the lake were being lost forever. The sons of the boatmen were becoming serfs of the land; the grandsons went armed with rocks to throw at their grandfathers; on the lake could be seen great barges laden with coal, while the rice fields extending in every direction, were invading the lake, devouring the water, and were already gnawing at the forest, cutting wide swaths in it. Ay, Lord! To behold all this, to witness the destruction of a world that he had looked upon as eternal! It would be better to die!

Isolated from his own, with no love other than the deep affection he felt for his mother, the Albufera, he would inspect it, review it daily, as if in his eyes, the keen, astute eyes of an old man, he was storing up all the water of the lake and the countless trees of the Dehesa.

They did not hew down a pine in the forest without his noting it at once from a great distance, from the center of the lake. Another one! .... The gap that the fallen tree left in the foliage of the trees near-by filled him with anguish, as if he were gazing into the hollow of a grave. He cursed the lessees of the Albufera,—insatiable thieves. The people of Palmar stole wood from the forest, it was true; in their hearths burned only twigs and branches of the Dehesa, they were satisfied with the dead wood, with the withered and fallen trunks; but these invisible gentlemen, who appeared only by proxy, in the guards' carbines and the tricks of the law, struck down with the greatest nonchalance the veterans of the forest,— giants that had gazed down upon him when as a youngster he crawled about the boats, and which were already huge trees when his father, the first Paloma, dwelt in a savage Albufera, killing with cane-stalks the snakes that swarmed on the river-bank,—more agreeable creatures than the men of nowadays.

In his sadness before the downfall of ancient customs and views, he sought the wildest spots of the lake,— those to which the anxieties of exploitation had not yet come.

The sight of an old water-wheel would send a shudder up his spine, and with deep emotion he contemplated the black, decayed wheel, the chipped buckets, filled with straw, out of which some rats jumped as he approached. These were the ruins of the dead Albufera; they were the souvenirs, as he himself was, of a better time.

When he wished to rest he landed on the plain of

Sancha, with its lagoons of jelly-like water and its high beds of rushes; here he would contemplate the green, somber landscape, in which there still seemed to quiver the sounds of the legendary monster's tightening coils, and he rejoiced to think that there yet existed something that was free from the voracity of modern men,—among whom he could count, ay! his son.

III

WHEN Tío Paloma desisted from the rude, strenuous education of his grandson, the latter breathed more easily.

He was tired of accompanying his father to the fields of Saler, and thought uneasily of his future when he beheld Tòni deep in the mud of the rice plantations, amid leeches and toads, his feet wet and his body burned by the sun. His lazy instincts then revealed themselves. No; he would not follow in his father's footsteps; he would not work the fields. To be a carabineer and stretch out at ease on the beach, or to be a civil guard such as those who came from Ruzafa with the yellow belts and the white queues seemed to him far preferable to cultivating rice, sweating in the water with one's legs swollen by bites.

The first few times that he had accompanied his grandfather through the Albufera he had found the life much to his taste. He liked to wander about the lake, to sail without any fixed goal, passing from one canal to another, or stopping in the middle of the lake to converse with the fishermen. Sometimes he would leap to the little islands of sedge and excite the lonely bulls with his whistling. At other times, he would enter the Dehesa, pick berries in the brambles, and poke the rabbit burrows, hunting for a young rabbit inside. His grandfather would applaud him when he would catch a *fòcha* or a *collvert* asleep between

50

wind and water, making it his own with certain aim.

He was fond, too, of lying on his back in the boat for hours, listening to his grandfather tell tales of long ago. Tìo Paloma recalled the most notable events of his life; his conversations with the great; certain smuggling expeditions of his early youth when he was shot at; and going still further back in his memories, he spoke of his father, the first Paloma, repeating what the latter had in his day told to him.

This boatman of olden days had also seen great things without ever having left the place. And Tío Paloma told his grandson about the trip made by Carlos IV and his queen to the Albufera, long before he himself had been born. This did not prevent Tonet from describing the large tents that had been set up among the pines of the Dehesa for the royal banquet, floored with costly carpets and topped with pennants; the music, the packs of hounds, the lackeys in powdered wigs in charge of the provision carts. The King dressed as a hunter, surrounded himself with Albufera's rustic marksmen, almost naked, and carrying old arquebuses; he admired their prowess while Maria Luisa strolled through the leafy woods arm in arm with Don Manuel Godoy.

And the old man, recalling that famous visit, wound up by singing the verses that his father had taught him:

> Debajo de un pino verde
> le dijo la reina al rey:
> "Mucho te quiero, Carlitos,
> pero más quiero á Manuel."[1]

[1] (Beneath a green pine-tree
The queen said to the king:
"I am fond of you, my Charley,
But it is Manuel that I love.")

His quivering voice, as he sang, assumed a malicious expression, and he accompanied every verse with sly winks, as if it were only a few days before that the folk of Albufera had made up the stanza in revenge for an expedition which, with all its pomp, seemed to insult the passive misery of the fishermen.

But this epoch, so joyous to Tonet, was of short duration. His grandfather began to be exacting and tyrannical with him. Seeing that the boy had become expert in managing the boat, he no longer allowed him to wander about as he liked. Mornings he would capture him and make him go fishing with him. The boy would have to carry along the *mornells* of the previous night,—large net bags at the bottom of which the eels would be ensnared,—and lower them anew: work taxing his strength, forcing him to stand on the gunwale of the boat, his back burning in the fire of the sun.

His grandfather would watch the work without stirring to lend a hand. On the way back to town he would stretch himself out in the bottom of the boat like an invalid, leaving the steering to his grandson, who poled the boat like one exhausted.

The boatmen, from a distance, would salute the wrinkled head of Tío Paloma just visible over the gunwale. Clever old bird! How comfortably he spent the day! He took it as easy as the priest of Palmar while his poor grandson sweated and worked. The grandfather would reply, as seriously as a professor: "That's the way to learn! My father taught me the same way!"

Later on came spearing: wandering over the lake from sunset to sunrise, in the darkness of winter nights. Tonet would keep watch at the prow over the bunch of dry grasses that burned like a torch, throwing over the black waters a wide blood stain. The grandfather stood at the poop, grasping the *fitora*: a heavy iron fork with pointed prongs,—a terrible weapon,—which, once plunged could be withdrawn only at the cost of great effort and horrible destruction. The light penetrated to the bottom of the lake. There one could see the shell bed, the aquatic plants, a whole world of mystery, invisible during the day; the water was so transparent that the boat seemed to be float- ing in the air with no support whatever. The creatures of the lake, deceived by the light, would blindly cluster around the red brightness, and Tío Paloma,—zas!— never thrust his *fitora* into the waters without pulling out a big fish that lashed its tail desperately at the end of the sharp trident.

At first this fishing roused Tonet's enthusiasm; but little by little the sport grew to be slavery, and he began to hate the lake, gazing yearningly at the white cottages of Palmar, which stood out against the dark lines of the islands of sedge.

He looked back enviously to his earliest days, when all he had to do was go to school, and when he used to play about the streets, sometimes hearing the women tell one another what a handsome child he was, and congratulat- ing his mother.

There he had been master of his life. His sickly mother spoke to him with a pale smile, finding an excuse for all his pranks, and La Borda supported him with the meek- ness of the inferior creature admiring the strong. The gamins that swarmed about the cabins recognized him as their leader, and they would go in a gang along the canal bank, throwing stones at the ducks, who fled quacking amid the women's shouts and cries.

The break with his grandfather meant a return to his former indolence. No longer would he leave Palmar before dawn to remain on the lake until nightfall. The whole day was his very own in the town, where there remained no men other than the priest in the presbytery, the teacher in the school and the chief of the coast guards strutting along the banks with his fierce mustache and his red, toper's nose, while the women made nets before the cabin doors, leaving the street to the mercy of the little tots.

Tonet, emancipated from labor, renewed former friendships. He had two chums who had been born in cabins close to his own: Neleta and Sangonera.

The girl had no father, and her mother was an old eelwoman of the city market, who at midnight would load her baskets upon the barge called "the eel cart." In the afternoon she would return to Palmar, her soft, billowy, obese body exhausted by the daily journey and the quarrels and chafferings of the Fish Market. The poor woman would go to sleep before nightfall, so that she might get up with the stars and follow this abnormal life that left her no time to attend to her daughter. The latter grew up with no more care than she received from the neighbors, and especially Tonet's mother, who often gave her things to eat, as if she were her own daughter. But the girl was less docile than La Borda, and was far more eager to follow Tonet in his escapades than to remain for hours at a time learning the various points about net-weaving.

Sangonera bore the same nick-name as his father, the

most noted drunkard in all Albufera,—an old sot who seemed to have been shrivelled up by alcohol, for many years past. When he was left a widower, with little *Sangonereta*[1] as his only child, he gave himself up to drink, and the village folk, beholding how eagerly he sucked at his favorite beverages, compared him to a leech (sanguijela), thus creating his nick-name.

He would disappear from Palmar for weeks. From time to time it would be learned that he was tramping through the cities of the mainland begging from the wealthy farmers of Catarroja and Masanasa, and sleeping off his sprees in the straw-lofts. Whenever he spent much time in Palmar there would disappear during the night the net-bags hung up in the canals; the *mornells* would be emptied of eels before the owners arrived, and more than one neighbor, on counting his ducks, cried to heaven that one was missing. The coast guard would cough loudly and glance in Old Sangonera's direction, as if he were ready to pierce the drunkard's eyes with the points of his formidable mustache; but the drunkard protested, calling all the saints, for lack of more reliable testimony, to witness his innocence. It was the malevolence of the village folk, who were bent upon ruining him, as if he didn't have enough to bear with his poverty, which compelled him to live in the most wretched cabin of the place! And in order to placate the stern representative of the law, who more than once had drunk in his company, but who, outside of the tavern did not recognize anybody, he would go off again on a trip over the other shore of the Albufera, not returning to Palmar for several weeks.

[1] Little Sangonera.

His son refused to follow him on these expeditions. Born in a shanty, into which bread never came, he had been compelled from childhood to get his food by his wits, and rather than accompany his father he chose to separate from him, so as not to have to share with him the product of his own skill.

When the fishermen would sit down to a meal, they would catch sight of a gloomy shadow walking back and forth in front of the cabin door; finally it would take up a position at one side, its head lowered and its gaze directed within, like a young bull preparing to attack. This was Sangonereta, who would be meditating upon his hunger with a hypocritical expression of submissiveness and shame, while his roguish eyes sparkled with the desire to make off with everything before him.

The vision would produce an effect upon the families. Poor boy! And catching a half-gnawed coot bone, a piece of tench or a crumb that would be thrown to him, he would manage to satisfy his hunger from door to door. If he noticed the dogs call to one another with a muffled barking and dash toward any of the Palmar taverns, he would run along too, as if he were in the secret. It would be hunters who were making their *paella,* gentlemen from Valencia who had come to the lake to eat an *all y pebre*; and when the strangers, seated before the little tavern table, had to defend themselves, by kicks, between one spoonful and another, from the milling of the famished dogs, they would discover that they were being aided by the tattered urchin, who, as a result of his smiles and his frightening away of the fierce dogs, would at length appropriate the remnants of the meal. A guard had given him an old barracks cap; the magistrate of the town had presented him with the trousers of a huntsman who had drowned in the reeds; and his feet, always bare, were as strong as his hands were weak, for his hands had never touched the pole or the oar.

Sangonera, filthy, famished, forever thrusting his hand under his grimy cap to scratch furiously away at his head, enjoyed great prestige among the youngsters. Tonet was the stronger, and could easily thrash him, but none the less he recognized his own inferiority and did everything that Sangonera told him. It was the prestige of one who is able to live by his own wits, without asking aid of anyone. The younger element admired him with no uncertain envy at beholding him live a life free from the fears of paternal correction and free of all obligations. And besides, his mischief-making was fascinating, and the boys, who in their own cabins would get a good slap for the least fault, thought themselves more manly when they went in the company of that rascal, who looked upon everything as his own, and knew how to turn it to good advantage, never finding anything left in the canal boats without appropriating it.

He had declared war against the creatures of the air, since it required less labor to capture them than to catch those of the lake. He would hunt, with ingenious methods of his own devising, the so-called Moorish sparrows which infest the Albufera and are feared by the farmers as an evil pest because they devour a large part of the rice harvest. His best season was summer, when *fumarells* abounded,—little gulls of the lake, which he caught in a net.

In this work he was aided by Tío Paloma's grandson. They were partners in this business, as Tonet gravely

declared, and the two boys would spend hours watching
on the banks of the lake, pulling at the line and imprison-
ing the unwary birds in the net. When they had caught
a good supply, Sangonera, hardy traveler, would take the
road to Valencia, carrying the net-bag on his back, while
inside the *fumarells* flapped their dark wings and in their
desperate writhings showed their white paunches. The
rascal would pass along the streets near the Fish Market,
crying his birds, and the city gamins would run to purchase the *fumarells* and send them flying over the cross-
ways, with a line of twine tied to their legs.

On his return there would be trouble between the partners, and commercial rupture. It was impossible to get
any accounting from such a rogue. Tonet got tired of
thrashing Sangonera without receiving an *ochavo* of the
proceeds from the sale; but ever credulous and duped by
the rascal's wiles, he would return in quest of him to the
ramshackle, doorless cabin where he slept alone for the
greater part of the year.

When Sangonera passed his eleventh year he began to
abandon his little friends. His parasitical instinct made
him frequent the church, since this was the most direct
road by which to introduce himself into the vicar's home.
In a town like Palmar the priest was as poor as any of
the fishermen, but Sangonera was tempted by the com-
munion wine which he had heard highly praised in the
taverns. Besides, during the summer days, when the lake
boiled beneath the sun, the little church seemed to him like
an enchanted palace, with its shadowy light filtering
through the green windows, its whitewashed walls and
the pavement of red stones exhaling the dampness of the
marshy soil.

Tío Paloma, who despised the rogue because he was an enemy of the boating-life, received the news of his new affiliations with disgust. Ah, the shameless tramp! How well he knew his business!

When the vicar would go to Valencia, the rascal would carry to the boat the wide kerchief, one of those known as herb kerchiefs, filled with clothes, and he would follow the craft along the banks, taking such affectionate farewell of the priest that one would imagine he was never to see him again. He helped the curate's servant with the household chores; he would fetch wood from the Dehesa, and water from the springs that rose in the lake, and he would be as excited as a hungry cat expecting dainties when, in the tiny room that served as the sacristy, alone and in silence, he would devour the food left over on the vicar's table. Mornings, pulling at the rope of the bell that awoke the town, he felt proud of his position. The encouraging pats on the shoulder with which the vicar encouraged his activities seemed to him signs of distinction that placed him above his companions.

But this desire to dwell in the shadow of the church would at times grow weak, yielding to some nostalgia for his former vagabond life. Then he would hunt up Neleta and Tonet, and together they would again take up their games and make forays along the banks, going as far as the Dehesa, which to his simple companions seemed the end of the world.

One autumn afternoon Tonet's mother sent them to the forest for wood. Instead of bothering her with their noisy play inside the cabin, they could be useful to her, fetching her some faggots, since winter was approaching.

The three went on the trip. The Dehesa was in blossom.

and as fragrant as a garden. The bushes, under the caress of a sun that was as warm as in summer, were full of flowers, and above them insects shone bright as gold, flitting about with a subdued buzzing. The twisted, age-less pines stirred with a stately murmur, and under the vaults formed by their wide tops a soft shade prevailed, like the shadows in the naves of an immense cathedral. From time to time a sunbeam fell between two tree-trunks, as if coming in through a window.

Tonet and Neleta, whenever they penetrated into the Dehesa, felt dominated by the same emotion. They were afraid, without knowing of what or of whom, imagining themselves in the enchanted palace of an invisible giant who might show himself at any moment.

They sauntered along over the winding paths of the forest, now hidden by the foliage that waved above their heads, now reaching the crest of a dune, from which, through the colonnade of trunks, could be seen the vast mirror of the lake, speckled by boats as tiny as flies.

Their feet slipped along the ground, which was cov-ered with moss. At the sound of their steps, at the least of their shouts, the thickets would quiver with the mad running of invisible creatures. They were rabbits taking to flight. From afar sounded drowsily the bells of the cows which were grazing off in the direction of the sea.

The youngsters seemed to be intoxicated by the calm and the perfumes of that serene afternoon. When, on winter days, they entered the forest the leafless, solitary thickets, the east wind that blew from the sea and froze their hands, the tragic look of the Dehesa in the gray light of a clouded sky made them gather their bundles of wood quickly on the very fringe of the forest and run all the way back to Palmar. But on that afternoon they went ahead confidently, eager to chase through the entire wood, even if they reached the end of the world.

One surprise followed another. Neleta, with her feminine instincts of self-adornment, instead of looking for dry wood cut off twigs of myrtle, waving them above her tangled hair. Afterward she gathered twigs of mint and other fragrant plants, covered with flowerets, which intoxicated her with their pungent perfume. Tonet picked wild bluebells, and weaving a garland of them, he arranged it over Neleta's dishevelled hair, laughing to see how closely she resembled the cherubs painted upon the altars of the church at Palmar. Sangonera searched everywhere, like a glutton, for something profitable amid this glorious, perfumed nature. He swallowed the red clusters of shepherd's cherries, and with a strength born only of hunger, he tore up from the ground the palmetto roots, looking for the *margalló*, the bitter stalk in whose pulpy folds he found the tender, sweet-tasting palm-seed.

In the bare spots of the forest, called *mallaes*,—low lands denuded of trees because they were submerged under water during the winter, fluttered the darning-needles and butterflies. As the children ran along they were pricked by the brambles and torn by the reeds, which were as sharp as lances, but they laughed at the smarting pain and ran on their way, amazed by the forest's beauty. On the paths they always found short worms, thick and bright-colored, as if they were animated flowers crawling along with nervous undulation. They picked up these caterpillars, admiring them as mysterious beings whose nature they could not guess, and then placed them back on the ground, crawling along on all fours after them, until they slowly wriggled into the thicket. The dragon-flies sent them scurrying here and there, and all three admired the nervous darting of the most common, red type, called *caballets,* and of the *marotas,* attired like fairies, with wings of silver, green backs and breasts covered with gold.

Wandering at random through the middle of the forest, farther than they had ever penetrated before, they noticed all at once that the look of the landscape was changing. They had plunged into the thickest of the glens until they found themselves in a twilight gloom. An incessant roar kept sounding ever nearer. It was the sea, lashing the beach on the other side of the chain of dunes which bounded the horizon.

The pines were not straight and imposing like those on the lake side. Their trunks were twisted; the foliage was almost white and the crowns bent downward. All the trees grew obliquely in the same direction, as if an invisible tempest were blowing amid the deep calm of the afternoon. The wind from the sea, during the great storms, tortured this side of the forest, giving it a funereal aspect.

The children turned back. They had heard of this part of the Dehesa, the most savage and dangerous section of the forest. The silence and the motionless thickets filled them with fear. Here it was that the big snakes ran into hiding when chased by the guards of the Dehesa; it was here that the wild bulls which strayed from the flock went grazing, obliging the hunters to load their muskets with coarse salt so as to frighten them without killing them.

Sangonera, as the one who was best acquainted with

the Dehesa, guided his party toward the lake, but the palmettos that he found on the road forced him to turn aside. until he lost his way. The afternoon was drawing to a close and Neleta grew scared when she saw the forest darken. The two boys laughed at her. The pines formed a huge house: it grew dark there as it did in their cabins, long before the sunset, but outside of the forest there still remained an hour of daylight. There was no hurry. And they continued their search for *margallóns*. The girl was calmed by the palm-seeds that Tonet gave her, and which she sucked at as she lingered on the way. Whenever she found herself alone at a bend in the road, she would run to catch up with them.

Now night was really falling. . . . Sangonera, as one who knew the Dehesa intimately, said so. No longer did the sound of the herd bells come from afar. They must get quickly out of the forest, but not before gathering some wood, so that they should not be scolded when they returned home. At the foot of the pines, among the bushes, they hunted for dry twigs. Hurriedly they made three small bundles, and almost gropingly set out on their way. They had gone only a few steps when darkness was complete. About where the lake of Albufera should be there was a glow like that of a huge fire on the point of dying down, but within the forest the trunks and the bushes barely stood out, deeper shadows against the fearsome background.

Sangonera lost his serenity, uncertain where they were going. They had strayed from the road; they blundered into thorny bushes that scratched their legs. Neleta sobbed with fear, and suddenly cried out and fell. She had stumbled against the roots of a pine tree that had been hewn close to the ground, and had hurt her foot. Sangonera suggested going ahead and leaving behind that cry-baby who could only whine. The girl choked back her tears, as if she were afraid of disturbing the silence of the forest, and attracting the horrible beasts that lived in the darkness, and Tonet, under his breath, threatened Sangonera with fabulous numbers of thrashings if he did not stay with them as their guide.

They walked along slowly, feeling out each step ahead until suddenly they no longer stumbled upon bushes, coming out on the slippery moss of the paths. But then, Tonet, in speaking, got no reply from his boy companion, who had been walking ahead.

"Sangonera! Sangonera!"

A noise of broken branches, of bushes scraped in flight, as if a wild animal were making his escape, was the only reply. Tonet shouted with rage. Oh, the big scoundrel! He had fled to get out of the forest sooner: he did not want to stay with his chums and have to help Neleta.

Left by themselves, the two children felt the sudden collapse of the little confidence they had in themselves. Sangonera, with his vagabond experience, had seemed to them a great help. Neleta, terrified, and forgetful of all prudence, wailed hysterically, and her cries resounded through the silence of the wood, which seemed so vast. His chum's fear aroused Tonet's energy. Then he had put his arm around the girl's shoulder, held her up, encouraged her, and asked her if she were able to walk, if she were willing to follow him, and they had kept on and on, though the poor fellow did not know where they were going.

For a long time they stuck together; she sobbing, he

trembling before the unknown, but determined to overcome it.

Something sticky and cold brushed by their faces; perhaps a bat; and this touch, which sent a shudder coursing through them, woke them from their depressing inertia. They began to walk hurriedly along, stumbling and getting up, becoming entangled in the bushes, bumping into trees, trembling at the sounds that spurred them on in their flight. The two thought of the same thing, but instinctively they concealed their thoughts from each other so as not to add to their fear. The recollection of Sancha was fixed in their memory. Before their mind's eye passed in rapid procession all the legends of the lake that they had heard at night beside the cabin hearth, and as their hands struck against the trunks they imagined that they had touched the wrinkled, icy skin of huge reptiles. The cries of the coots sounding from afar in the sedge of the lake, seemed to them the groans of murdered people. Their mad careening through the bushes, snapping off twigs, trampling over plants, disturbed mysterious creatures who also ran through the underbrush kicking up the dry leaves.

They reached a wide clearing, without being able to determine in just what part of the interminable wood they were. In this open space the darkness was not so intense. Above extended the sky, of a deep blue, shimmering with light, like a vast canvas stretched above the black masses of the forest that surrounded the plain. The two youngsters stopped in this luminous, tranquil island. They felt powerless to go any farther. They trembled with fear before the deep grove that moved on all sides like a tide of black waves.

They sat down, tightly clutching each other, as if the contact of their bodies inspired them with confidence. Neleta no longer was crying. Exhausted with pain and fatigue, she leaned her head against her friend's shoulder, groaning faintly. Tonet looked in every direction, as if, more than by the gloom of the wood, he were frightened in that crepuscular light, in which every moment he imagined he beheld the silhouette of some wild beast, the foe of strayed children. The song of the cuckoo broke the silence; the frogs of a near-by pool, which had stopped croaking as soon as the children arrived, recovered their confidence and returned to their sing-song; the persistent, bothersome mosquitos buzzed about their heads, their wings gleaming a little in the dark twilight.

Little by little the two children recovered their calm. It was not at all bad there: they might spend the night in that place. And the warmth of their bodies, pressed tightly to each other, seemed to give them new life, causing them to forget the fear and the mad dashing through the wood.

Above the pines, in the direction of the sea, the space began to be tinted with a whitish light. The stars seemed to go out, submerged in a wave of milk. The children, excited by the mysterious environment of the wood, watched this phenomenon with awe, as if someone were flying down to their aid in an aureole of light. The pine branches, with the thready texture of their foliage, stood out against a luminous background as if sketched in black. A shining object began to appear above the tree-tops: at first it was a slightly curved line, like a silver eyebrow; then it became a dazzling semi-circle, and at last, a huge face, of soft, honey color, which dragged along through the neighboring stars its splendrous head of hair. The moon seemed to smile down upon the two children, who contemplated it with the adoration of little savages.

With the appearance of this chubby-cheeked countenance the wood became transformed; the rushes of the plain shone like silver fans. At the foot of each tree was a restless black spot, and the forest seemed to grow, to duplicate itself, a second shadowy grove extending over the bright ground. The *buxqueròts,* wild nightingales of the lake, and such intense lovers of their liberty that they die almost as soon as they are put into a cage, burst into song throughout the clearing, and even the mosquitoes buzzed more melodiously in the space that was drenched in light.

The two children began to find their adventure pleasant. Neleta no longer felt any pain in her foot and she whispered softly into her companion's ear. Her precocious feminine instinct, her craftiness, like that of an abandoned and wandering kitten, made her superior to Tonet. They would remain in the wood, wouldn't they? The next day, when they returned to the town, they would make up some reason for their adventure. Sangonera would be blamed. They would spend the night there, seeing things they had never seen; they would sleep together: they would be like man and wife. And in their ignorance they trembled as they uttered these words, clutching their arms even more tightly. They hugged each other, as if their instincts told them that their growing affection required the blending of their bodies' warmth.

Tonet felt a strange, inexplicable intoxication. Never had the body of his playmate, which he had more than

once beaten in their rude games, possessed for him that
sweet warmth which seemed to spread through his veins
and rise to his head, causing the same light-headedness as
the glasses of wine his grandfather used to offer him in
the tavern. He gazed vaguely ahead of him, but his entire attention was concentrated on Neleta's head against
his shoulder; on the caressing touch of her breath on his
neck, as if a velvety hand were tickling him. The two
were silent, and their silence added to the enchantment.
She opened her green eyes, in whose depths the moon was
reflected like a dewdrop, and turning so as to find a more
comfortable position, closed them again.

"Tonet . . . . Tonet," she murmured, as if in a dream;
and she pressed closer to her companion.

What time was it? . . . The boy felt his eyes closing,
not so much with sleep as from the strange intoxication
that seemed to overwhelm him. Of the forest murmurs
he could now make out only the buzzing of the mosquitoes,
fluttering like a nimbus of shadow above the hard skins
of the lake children. Some of them screeched like stri-
dent violins, prolonging the same note infinitely; others,
more grave, played a short scale, and the big ones droned
with a muffled vibration, like bass-viols or the far-off
tolling of a bell.

On the following morning they were awakened by the
sun burning their faces, and the barking of a guardsman's
dog which had thrust his jaws close to their eyes.

They were almost on the boundary of the Dehesa, and
the distance to Palmar was very short.

Tonet's mother, usually so kind and sad, reimbursing
herself for a night of anxiety, ran at him, stick in hand,
and struck him several blows in spite of his swift agility.

In addition, by way of advance payment until Neleta's mother should arrive on the "eel cart," she cuffed and slapped the girl so that she would not get lost in the woods another time.

After this adventure the entire town, with tacit agreement, called Tonet and Neleta sweethearts. And the two, as if forever bound by that night of innocent proximity spent in the wood, sought each other out and loved each other without asserting it in so many words, as if it were thoroughly understood that they could belong only to each other. This episode spelled the end of their childhood. Gone were now their forays, their happy, carefree life exempt from all obligations. Neleta followed the same career as her mother: every night she would leave for Valencia, with the eel baskets, and she would not return until the following afternoon. Tonet, who could see her for only a moment at nightfall, worked on his father's fields, or went fishing with his grandfather.

Tío Tòni, formerly so lenient, was now as exacting as Tío Paloma, seeing that his son had grown up, and Tonet, like a resigned beast, let himself be dragged to work. His father, that obstinate hero of the soil, was not to be shaken in his determination. When the season for planting rice arrived, or the harvest time, the boy would spend all his days in Saler. The rest of the year he would fish in the lake, sometimes with his father, at others with his grandfather, who admitted him on board as his comrade, but who every moment swore against the beastly luck that had let such tramps be born into the family.

Moreover, the boy was impelled to work by boredom. There was nobody left in town for him to play with during the day. Neleta was in Valencia, and his

former playmates, now like himself grown up and obliged
to earn their own living, went off in their fathers' boats.
Sangonera was left; but that ragamuffin, after the adventure in the Dehesa, kept aloof from Tonet, keeping in
mind the cudgelling he had received as a reward for his
defection of that night.

The little tramp, as if this event had determined his future, had taken refuge in the priest's house, helping his
servant, sleeping like a dog behind the door, without
thinking of his father, who appeared only from time to
time in his abandoned shack through the roof of which
the rain fell as freely as in the open fields.

Old Sangonera now had a trade: when he wasn't drunk
he devoted himself to hunting the otters of the lake, which
having been unremittingly pursued for centuries, did not
number a dozen in all.

One afternoon when he lay on a bank digesting his
wine, he had seen the water begin to whirl and seethe
with large bubbles. Somebody was diving deep, among
the nets that stretched across the canal, looking for the
mornells loaded with fish. Once in the water, with a pole
that they let him take, he began to pursue with swift jabs
a blackish animal that made for bottom until he slew it
and took possession of it.

It was the famous *lludria,* which was spoken of in Palmar as a fantastic animal; the otter which in former days
swarmed in the lake in such numbers that it made fishing
impossible, breaking all the nets.

The old vagabond now considered himself the first
man of the Albufera. The Society of Fisherman of Palmar, according to ancient statutes inscribed in the huge
tomes in the custody of their head, the Warden, was

pledged to give a *duro* for each otter presented to them.
The old man took his reward, but did not stop there. That
animal was a treasure; and he began to exhibit it in the
harbor of Catarroja, then at Silla, reaching as far as
Sueca and Cullera in his triumphant trip around the lake.

He was in great demand. There wasn't a tavern where
they didn't receive him with open arms. "Come right in
Tío Sangonera! Let's see the big fellow you landed!"
And the vagabond, after having himself treated to several
glasses, would lovingly draw forth from under his coat
the poor creature, whitish and foul-smelling, displaying its
skin for the admiration of the spectators and letting them
pass their hands across it—but very carefully, remember!
—so that they might appreciate the fineness of its hair.

Never had little Sangonereta, when he first came into
this world, been carried with more affectionate tenderness
in the arms of his father, than was that creature. But
with the passing of the days, folks tired of the *lludria,*
nobody offered even a glass of bad whisky for the sight
of it, and there wasn't a tavern that did not chase Sangonera out as if he had the plague, because of the insuffer-
able stench from the putrefying animal he carried everywhere under his cloak. Before abandoning it, however,
he made fresh profit from it, selling it in Valencia to a
dissecter of animals, and since then he had told everybody
about his vocation: he was going to be an otter hunter.

He now devoted himself to the quest of another otter,
like one in pursuit of happiness. The reward given by
the Society of Fishermen, and the week of continuous
drunken hilarity at the expense of others, on a royal spree,
could not leave his memory. But the second otter would
not consent to be caught. Sometimes he imagined he

saw it in one of the remotest spots of the lake, but at once it would hide, as if the entire lake family had passed the word along about Old Sangonera's new profession. His despair caused him to get drunk on the otters that he expected to catch, and he had already gulped down two of them, when one night some fishermen found him drowned in a canal. He had slipped in the mire, and unable to pick himself up, because he was dead drunk, he remained in the water forever watching for his otter.

The death of Sangonera's father caused him to take refuge in the vicar's home; never did he return to the shanty. One curate succeeded another in Palmar, which was a punishment town, where only the hopeless ones came, or those who were in disgrace, and they escaped as soon as they could. All the vicars, on taking possession of the poor little church, took Sangonera over with it as if he were something necessary to the ritual. In all the town he was the only one who could assist at mass. He had at his fingertips all the things kept in the sacristy, with the number of rips, patches and moth-holes they had; he was so solicitous and eager to please in everything that no sooner did his master express a desire than it was at once fulfilled.

The fact that he was the only male of the town who did not labor with a pole in hand or spend his night in the middle of the Albufera, filled him with a certain pride, and made him look disdainfully and haughtily down upon everybody else.

Sundays, at daybreak, it was he who led the procession, holding the cross high, in front of the rosary. Men, women and children, in two long rows, went singing along in leisurely fashion, through the only street of the village, afterwards turning aside to the banks and the isolated cabins so that the ceremony might take longer. In the scant light of the dawn the canals gleamed like sheets of dark steel, the clouds in the direction of the sea were tipped with red and the Moorish sparrows wheeled in flocks, rising from the roofs of the eel-ponds, answering the sad melancholy song of the faithful with their merry chirping of contented nomads.

"Christian, awake!" . . . . sang the procession through the town; and the comical part about the call was that the entire population was in the procession, and in the empty houses, only the dogs awoke with their barking, and the roosters, who broke in upon the sad chant with their crowing, as sonorous as a trumpet, saluting the dawn and the joy of another day.

Tonet, as he marched along in the row, glared with rage at his former chum, leading them all like a general, bearing the cross aloft like a banner. Ah, the scoundrel! He knew how to live a life to his taste!

And he, in the meantime, lived in submission to his father, who was daily growing graver and less communicative: good at bottom, but becoming cruelty itself toward his own family in his tenacious passion for work. The times were bad. The lands of Saler were not giving good harvest, and usury, to which Tío Tòni had had recourse to aid his undertakings, devoured the greater part of his efforts. At fishing, the Palomas always had bad luck, drawing the worst locations in the lake in the community allotments. Then there was the mother, slowly fading away; she was living in the death-agony, as if life were melting her down like a burning candle, with no other light than the sickly glow of her eyes.

It was a sad existence that Tonet now led. No longer did he stir Palmar with his escapades; no longer did the women neighbors kiss him and call him the handsomest boy in the town; no longer was he the one to be selected, on the day the *redolins* (fishing sites) were drawn for, to put his hand into the leather bag of the Society and draw out the names. Now he was a man. Instead of his desires predominating in the home, as they had done when he was a pampered child, he was now ordered about; he counted as little as did La Borda, and at the slightest sign of rebellion, Tío Tòni's hand would rise menacingly, while the grandfather approved with shrill laughter, affirming that such was the way to bring up children.

When the mother died, the old affection between the grandfather and the boy seemed to be born anew. Tío Paloma deplored the absence of that docile creature who suffered all his whims in silence; he felt a vacuum about him, and seized upon his grandson, never very willingly obedient, but never daring to be contrary and stubborn in his presence.

They went fishing together, as they had done in the olden days; they would pass an hour at the tavern like comrades, while in the cabin poor La Borda would attend to the household duties with that precocity characteristic of undesirable creatures.

Neleta, too, was like one of the family. Her mother was no longer able to go to the Valencia market. The dampness of the Albufera seemed to have penetrated into her very marrow, paralyzing her body, and the poor woman lay motionless in her hut, groaning from rheumatic pains, howling like one of the damned, and unable to make a living. Her market companions would give

Cuba, and a carabineer in Spain; afterward he had lived many years in Algeria: he had been a jack-of-all-trades and knew so much—so much!—as Tío Paloma said, that while he slept he discovered where every *peseta* was hiding, and on the following day he would run and get it.

Never had such wine as his been drunk in Palmar. The best of everything in that house! The owner received his customers pleasantly and charged a fair price.

Cañamèl was not a native of Palmar, nor even a Valencian. He came from far off, where the language was Castillian. In his youth he had been to the Albufera as a carabineer, and had married a poor, ugly girl of Palmar. After a wandering life, having accumulated a little money, he had come to settle down in his wife's town, yielding to her desires. The poor woman was sick and showed little signs of life: she seemed to have been exhausted by all those journeys that had caused her to yearn for her peaceful corner of the lake.

The other inn-keepers of the place inveighed against Cañamèl when they saw how he was taking their customers away. The big scoundrel! Not without reason did he give such good wine at such low prices! What least interested him was his tavern: his real business was elsewhere, and there was a reason, too, for his having come from such a distance to settle down there. But Cañamèl, when he learned of these words, smiled genially. After all, everybody had to live!

Cañamèl's most intimate friends knew that these rumors were not without foundation. The tavern was only a drop in the bucket. His principal business was practised at night, after closing the tavern. Not for nothing had he been a carabineer and patrolled the shores. Every month bales fell upon the coast, rolling over the sand, pushed by a swarm of dark forms who picked them up and carried them across the Dehesa to the shores of the lake. There, the large vessels, the *laúdes*[1] of Albufera, which could take on a cargo of a hundred sacks of rice, loaded themselves with the bales of tobacco, slowly setting sail through the darkness for the mainland. . . . And on the following day, not a trace of anything.

For these expeditions he chose the bravest of the men who frequented his tavern. Tonet, despite his few years, was favored two or three times with Cañamèl's confidence because he was a valiant, discreet boy. In this nocturnal toil a good man could earn two or three *duros,* which afterward he returned to Cañamèl in the tavern, drinking his wine. Yet the wretched fellows, commenting the following day on the hazards of an expedition in which they had been the chief protagonists, would say to one another in wonderment: "What courage this Cañamèl has! . . . . How boldly he exposes himself to the clutches of the law! . . . ."

Things were going well. On the beach, all were blind, thanks to the tavern-keeper's cleverness. His former friends of Algiers sent him his cargoes punctually, and the business rolled along so smoothly, that Cañamèl, despite the fact that he paid very generously for the silence of those who could harm him, prospered rapidly. After a year's residence in Palmar he had already bought up rice lands and in the upper story of the tavern he had his sack of silver to help out those who came for loans.

His importance grew by leaps and bounds. At the be-

---

[1] Tombstones.

ginning they had nick-named him *Cañamèl* because of the soft, sweet voice in which he spoke a labored Valencian. Afterwards, seeing him grown wealthy, without forgetting his nick-name, they took to calling him Paco, since, as his wife said, they called him that in his own birthplace; and if they ever nick-named him Quico, as they did all the other Franciscos of the locality, he became furiously sullen.

When his wife, the wretched companion of his struggling days, died, her elder sister, an ugly fisherwoman, a widow of domineering character, tried to camp in the tavern as its overseer, escorted by all the other members of her family. They flattered Cañamèl with all the attentions inspired by a wealthy relative, telling him how hard it was for a man to attend to the tavern unaided. A woman was needed there! But Cañamèl, who had always detested his sister-in-law for her sharp tongue, and trembled at the possibility that she might aspire to take the still warm place of her sister, showed her the door, defying her scandalous protestations. For the care of the tavern two old women, the widows of fishermen, sufficed; they cooked the *all y pebres* for the gourmands who came from Valencia, and wiped off the bar against which the entire populace wore out their elbows.

Cañamèl, finding himself free, spoke against matrimony. A man with a fortune like his could marry only for convenience,—some woman who had more money than he. And at night he would laugh to hear Tío Paloma, who grew eloquent when he discoursed upon women.

The old boatman declared that a man should be like

the *buxqueròts* of the lake, who sing merrily as long as they are at liberty, but who, when shut up, prefer death to being caged.

All his comparisons were provided by the birds of the Albufera. Women! . . . A pestiferous tribe! They were the most ungrateful, forgetful creatures in all creation. All you had to do was look at the *collvèrts* of the lake. They always fly in company with the female, and never go anywhere or hunt a meal without her. The hunter shoots. If the female falls dead, the poor male, instead of taking to flight, hovers and hovers above the spot until the huntsman dispatches him, too. But if it's the poor male that falls, the female continues to fly gaily on, without turning her head, as if nothing had happened, and when she notices that her mate is missing, she looks for another . . . Christ! That's the way all females are, whether they wear feathers or skirts.

Tonet would pass his nights playing *truque* in the tavern, waiting anxiously for Sunday, so that he might spend the entire day there. He liked this idle life, with his jug within reach, shuffling the grimy cards over the cloth that covered the table, and betting with little pebbles or corn seeds that represented the amount of the wagers. Too bad he was not rich, like Cañamèl, so he could devote himself entirely to this lordly life! He fumed when he thought that on the following day he would have to be working like a horse in the boat, and his passion for idling became so great that Cañamèl no longer sought him out for the nocturnal expeditions, noticing with what a wry face he carried the bales and how he disputed with his co-laborers to avoid work.

He exhibited activity and shook off his somnolent indolence only at the prospect of an approaching diversion. During the great festivities in Palmar, in honor of the Infant Jesus, on the third day of Christmas week, Tonet distinguished himself among all the youths of the lake. When, on the eve of the feast the musicians arrived from Catarroja on a large boat, the youths ran into the water of the canal, fighting in the race out to seize the bass-drum. This was an honor, which gave the young men a chance to strut proudly before the maidens—to get possession of the huge instrument, place it on one's back and parade it through the town.

Tonet plunged almost up to his waist in the water, which was as cold as ice; he disputed first place with the boldest of the youths, and climbing up the gunwale of the vessel, made the huge drum his own.

Later, during the three holidays, came the stormy diversions which ordinarily wound up with blows. There was the ball in the square, by the light of resinous torches, where he obliged Neleta to remain seated, since she was not his sweetheart for nothing, while he danced with other less good-looking, but better-dressed girls; then there were the nights of the *albaes,* serenades given by the younger element, who went from door to door until daybreak, singing verses, guarding a skin of wine that replenished their strength, and accompanying each song with one salvo of cat-calls and another of shots.

But after this season passed by, Tonet again began to feel bored with his life of toil, bounded by the horizon of the lake. At times he would defy his father's anger and escape, disembarking in the harbor of Catarroja and making a tour of the inland towns, where he had friends

during the harvest season. At other times he would take
the road to Saler, and would arrive at Valencia, fully
intending to remain permanently in the city, until hunger
sent him back again to the cabin of his father. He had
seen near at hand the life of those who live without
toil, and was disgusted with his wretched lot which forced
him to remain like an amphibian in a land of reeds and
mud, where man, from his earliest days, has to shut himself in a tiny craft,—an eternal coffin without which he
could not move around.

The hunger for pleasures arose in him,—a ravenous,
dominating passion. He gambled at the tavern until
Cañamèl would throw him out at midnight; he had tested
all the drinks that are used in Albufera, including the
pure absinthe that the hunters bring from the city to mix
with the vile-tasting water of the lake; and more than
one night, when he stretched himself out on his bed, his
father's eyes had followed him with a severe expression,
noting his uncertain step and his drunken, panting respiration. The grandfather protested indignantly. That
he should drink wine, all well and good; after all, they
were forever on the lake and a good boatman needs to
keep his stomach warm. . . . But *mixed* drinks?. . . .
That was how Old Sangonera had begun!

Tonet forgot all his affections. He beat La Borda,
treating her as if she were a submissive beast, and he
scarcely paid any attention to Neleta, receiving her words
with snorts of impatience. If he obeyed his father it
was in so churlish a manner that the industrious toiler
turned pale, his powerful hands twitching as if he were
aching to strangle his son. The youth looked down
upon the entire town, considering it a wretched herd, born

for hunger and fatigue, and out of whose ranks he must rise at all costs. Those who returned proudly from their day's fishing, exhibiting their baskets of eels and tenches, made him laugh. As he passed the vicar's house he could see Sangonera, who, now given up to reading, spent hours seated at the door perusing religious books and masking his rascally countenance with a sanctimonious air. Imbecile! What did he care for the old books that the vicar lent him? . . . .

He desired to live, to enjoy all the delights of existence at a time. He imagined that every person dwelling on the other side of the lake, in the wealthy towns or in the great, bustling city, was robbing him of the share of pleasures that was his by an indisputable right.

During the harvest season, when thousands of men came from all the corners of the province to the Albufera, attracted by the big pay offered for help by the proprietors, Tonet managed for a moment to reconcile himself to life in that corner of the world. He would see new faces, would make friends, and found a rare joy among these vagabonds, who, sickle in hand and a bundle of clothes slung over their shoulder, went from one place to another working while the sun shone, and getting drunk as soon as night fell.

He was fond of these fellows and their wandering lives, and their stories appealed to him as far more interesting than the fireside tales he had always heard. Some had been to America, and forgetting the wretchedness of their lives in those remote countries, spoke of them as of a paradise where everybody swam in gold. Others told of their long stays in wild Algeria, on the very outskirts of the desert, where for a long time they had been in hiding, because of a knife-thrust they had given in their home towns, or a robbery that had been "framed up" against them by their enemies. And Tonet, as he listened, imagined he could detect, in the vile-smelling breeze that blew over Albufera, the exotic perfume of those marvellous countries, and in the tiles of the tavern he could behold their fabulous wealth.

This friendship with the vagrant laborers became so close that, when the harvest was over and they had collected their pay, Tonet took part with them in a brutal orgy through the towns lying near the lake; a mad carousal from one wine-shop to another, of *albaes* sung at night before certain windows, and ending in a general brawl when, the money having given out, the wine began to taste rather sour and disputes arose as to whose turn it was to pay.

One of these expeditions became famous throughout Albufera. It lasted more than a week, and during all this time Tío Tòni did not see his son in Palmar. It was learned that the band of roisterers was running amuck like a wild beast over near Ribera, and that in Sollana they had cudgelled a guard, while in Sueca two of the gang had received cracked heads in a tavern squabble. The Civil Guard was despatched to take the crazy expedition in hand.

One night Tòni was informed that his son had just appeared at Cañamèl's place, his clothes all drenched in mud, as if he had fallen into a canal, and his eyes still burning from his seven-day spree. The sombre toiler went there, as silent as ever, with a barely perceptible snort that moved his lips as if they were stuck to each other.

His son was sitting in the middle of the tavern, drinking with the thirst of the drunkard, surrounded by an attentive public, which he filled with laughter at the account of the deviltries they had committed on this wild spree.

With a single blow Tío Tòni struck the jug that the youth was bringing to his lips, and sent it shattering to the floor, while the boy's head fell upon his shoulder. Tonet, thunderstruck by the blow, and beholding his father before him, for a moment or two recoiled; very soon, however, with a clouded, impure, terror-inspiring look in his eyes he rose to attack him, shouting that nobody would strike him and get away unpunished, not even his own father.

But it was no easy matter to resist that grave, silent giant, as firm as duty, who bore in his muscles the energy of more than thirty years of continuous battle wih poverty. Without opening his lips he dominated the wild beast that tried to bite him; with a blow that sent his son staggering, and, almost at the same time, with a kick he threw him against the wall, where he fell on his elbows across a table where some men were gambling.

The bystanders rushed upon the father to restrain him, but in his anger the silent giant would belabor every customer in the place. When calm had been restored and they let Tío Tòni go, his son was no longer there. He had fled, with his arms raised in an attitude of despair. . . . He had been thrashed! . . . . He, who was so much feared! . . . And in the presence of all Palmar! . . . .

Several days went by without any news from Tonet. Little by little it was discovered that he had gone to the

Valencian market. He was in the barracks of Monte-
Olivete, and very soon would embark for Cuba. He had
enlisted. Fleeing desperately toward the city, he had
stopped in some taverns near the barracks where the
recruiting banner for service across the sea had been
displayed. The men that were swarming there, volun-
teers waiting for embarkation and wily recruiting-offi-
cers, had induced him to take the step.

At the very first, Tío Tòni felt like protesting. The
boy was not yet twenty; the affair was illegal. Besides,
it was his son, his only son. But, with his habitual harsh-
ness, the grandfather induced him to let the matter go.
It was the best possible thing that could happen to the
grandson. He was growing up crooked: let him wander
about the world and suffer! They'd see to straightening
him out! And if he died, one tramp less: after all,
everybody had to die sooner or later.

The youth left without protest upon his father's part.
La Borda was the only one who, escaping from the
cabin, appeared at Monte-Olivete and weepingly said
good-bye to him, after giving him all his clothes and
whatever money she could scrape together without Tío
Tòni's knowledge. And not a word to Neleta: the youth
seemed to have forgotten her.

Two years went by without any signs of life from
Tonet. One day there came a letter for the father, opening with dramatic phrases, keyed in a false sentimentality,
in which Tonet asked his pardon, speaking then of his
new existence. He was a civil guard in Guantánamo,
and things were not so bad at all. In his style could be
noted a certain vainglorious air,—that of a man who

struts about the fields with his gun across his shoulder, scattering terror and inspiring respect. His health was excellent. Not the slightest illness ever since he had left. The men from the Albufera withstood the island climate with perfect ease. Anyone who had been brought up in that lake, drinking its muddy water, could fearlessly travel anywhere; he was acclimated.

Then came the Spanish-American war. In Tío Tòni's cabin La Borda went around trembling with fear, weeping in the corners whenever there arrived at Palmar confused news of the battles that were taking place far away. Two women of the town were wearing mourning. The youths, when they marched to the draft, did so to the accompaniment of desperate weeping, as if their families would never behold them again.

But Tonet's letters were tranquilizing, and exhibited great confidence. Now he was the head of a band of mounted guerrilla-fighters, and seemed well content with his existence. He described himself in great detail, as attired in striped cotton duck, with a wide Panama hat, patent-leather boots, his machete striking against his thighs, his mauser carbine across his shoulder and his belt filled with cartridges. He hadn't a care in the world; this was the life for him: good pay, plenty of action and the great freedom that danger permits. "Let the war come!" he said, merrily, in his letters. And one could easily conjure up the picture of the braggart soldier, content with his position, happy to suffer fatigue, hunger and thirst, in return for liberating himself from monotonous, commonplace toil, for living outside of the laws of normal times, for killing without fear of punishment and considering everything he looked upon as his own, imposing his will beneath the shelter of war's grim exigencies.

From time to time Neleta learned of her sweetheart's adventures. Her mother had died. She was now living in the cabin of one of her aunts, and earned her living by serving in Cañamèl's place on the days when special customers came and there were many *paellas* to see to.

She would come to the Paloma cabin and ask La Borda whether a letter had arrived; she would listen while it was read, with her eyes lowered and her lips pressed tightly together so as to concentrate all the more effectively. It seemed that her feelings for Tonet had grown cold ever since that flight, in which he showed no signs of having his sweetheart at all in mind. Her eyes would sparkle and she would smile, murmuring *grasies* (thanks) when, at the end of the letters the guerrilla-fighter would send his regards to her; but she showed no desire to have the youth return, nor was she enthusiastic when he built castles in the air, assuring them all that he would yet come back to Palmar in an officer's uniform.

Other matters were on Neleta's mind. She had become the most attractive girl in the Albufera. She was small, but her hair, bright blond, grew in such abundance that it formed upon her head a helmet of that ancient gold discolored by time. Her skin was white, of an almost transparent clarity, showing a delicate network of veins; such a skin had never been seen in the women of Palmar, whose scaly hide, of metallic glint, offered a distant resemblance to that of the tenches in the lake. Her eyes were small, of a cloudy green, shining like two drops of the absinthe the hunters from Valencia drank.

She frequented Cañamèl's place more and more. No longer did she lend her services only upon extraordinary occasions. She spent the entire day in the tavern, cleaning it, handing glasses over the counter, watching the fire where the pans bubbled, and when night came she would march off ostentatiously to her aunt's cabin, chaperoned by the latter, attracting universal attention, so that Cañamèl's hostile relatives might take due notice. Surely enough the relatives began to spread rumors that maybe Neleta saw the sun rise at her employer's side.

Cañamèl could not do without her. The widower, who up to that time had lived in peace with his old servants, publicly scorning all women, was unable to resist the contact with this designing little creature who rubbed against him with feline touch. Poor Cañamèl felt himself burn under the green eyes of that kitten, who scarcely beheld him at ease than she set about to rob him of his peace by skilful encounters that revealed her hidden charms. Her words and glances disturbed in the aging tavern-keeper a chastity of several years duration. The customers sometimes noticed that he had scratches on his face; at other times his eyes would be black and blue; and they would laugh at the confused excuses that the tavern-keeper would try to make. The little girl knew how to defend herself from Cañamèl's irresistible fits of passion! She set him afire with her eyes and extinguished him with her nails! At times, in the inner rooms of the place there would be heard the scraping of furniture, and the partitions would tremble with the impact of furious shoves, while the drinkers would laugh maliciously. . . . Cañamèl try-

ing to pet his cat! He'd certainly show up behind the
bar with a new scratch! . . . .

This struggle had to come to an end. Neleta was too
firm for the heavy-paunched fellow, who trembled when
she threatened never to return to the tavern, and at last
surrendered. All Palmar was stirred by the news of
Cañamèl's marriage to her, although it was something
they had long expected. The groom's sister-in-law went
from door to door, belching insults. The women formed
groups before the cabins. . . . The impudent little hussy!
How well she had gone about it to catch the wealthiest
man in Albufera! Nobody recalled her former affair with
Tonet. Six years had gone by since he had left, and
rarely did men return from the place he had gone to.

Neleta, when she took possession of the tavern as its
legitimate proprietress,—a place frequented by the whole
town and to which the needy came imploring loans from
Cañamèl,—did not swell up with pride, nor did she desire
to wreak vengeance upon the gossips who had slandered
her during the time she acted as servant. She treated
everybody kindly, but in order to avoid undue familiarity
she interposed the bar between herself and the women
visitors.

She no longer visited the cabin of the Palomas. She
treated La Borda as a sister when the latter came to purchase anything, and she served Tío Paloma his wine in the
largest glass they had, trying to forget his small debts.
Tío Tòni came very seldom to the tavern; but whenever Neleta saw him, she greeted him most respectfully,
as if that silent, preoccupied man were a parent that did
not care to own her, but whom she revered in secret.

These were the only affections of the past that survived

in her. She ran her establishment as if she had never
done anything else; she knew how to silence the drinkers
with a single word; her white arms, always with the
sleeves rolled up, seemed to attract persons from all the
banks of the Albufera; the business was progressing fa-
mously, and every day she seemed fresher, prettier,
prouder than ever, as if all at once her body had been
infused with all her husband's wealth, which was spoken
of with astonishment and envy throughout the lake dis-
trict.

On the other hand, Cañamèl seemed, in a way, to show
symptoms of decline soon after marriage. The health
and bloom of his wife seemed to be stolen from him.
Finding himself wealthy and married to the most beautiful girl in all Albufera, he seemed to think that now the
moment had come to get sick for the first time in his
life. Times were not favorable to the smuggling business; the young, inexperienced officers in charge of the
coast guard would not do business with him, and since
Neleta knew more about the tavern than Cañamèl,
the latter, not knowing what to do, decided to be an
invalid which is, according to Tío Paloma, a rich man's
luxury.

The old fellow knew better than anybody else what
the tavern-keeper's trouble was, and he spoke of it.
The amorous beast had been aroused in him, after having
lain dormant during the years when his only passion was
that of gain. Neleta exercised the same influence over
him that she had done when she was his servant. The
glitter of those two drops of her eyes, a smile, a word,
the touch of her arm as it met his while she filled the
glasses on the bar, were enough to go to his head. But

now Cañamèl received no scratches, nor were the customers scandalized when he left the counter. . . .

And in this way time went by. Cañamèl kept complaining of mysterious ailments; now his head would ache, now his stomach; he grew obese and flaccid, with billows of fat through which the degeneration of his organism could be guessed; and Neleta grew stronger day by day, as if the tavern-keeper's life, as it melted away drop by drop, fell into her veins like a regenerating stream.

Tío Paloma commented with comical gravity upon the situation. The race of the Cañamèls would reproduce so fruitfully that it would overrun all Palmar. But four years went by, and Neleta, despite her fervent desires, had not become a mother. She wanted a son, that her position might be assured, and also, as she said, to make the first wife's relatives burst with envy and rage. Every six months the news was bruited about in the town that she was pregnant, and when the women entered the tavern they would examine her with inquisitorial attention, fully aware of the importance such an event would have in the contest of the tavern-proprietress against her enemies. But always this hope foundered.

The moment it was supposed that Neleta was on the way to becoming a mother, the most atrocious rumors were set afloat concerning her. Her enemies thought maliciously of some of the rice-land owners that came from the towns of the Ribera and stopped over at the inn; of some hunter from Valencia; even of the lieutenant of the carabineers, who, bored in the solitude of Torre Nueva, would come once in a while and tie his horse to the olive tree before Cañamèl's place, after having crossed the mud of the canals: they thought, in fact, of anybody and everybody, except the sickly tavern-keeper, who was more than ever a prey to that insatiable passion which seemed to consume him.

Neleta would smile at the rumors. She did not love her husband; of that much she was certain: she felt a greater attraction for many who visited her tavern, but she possessed the prudence of the egotistic, foreseeing woman who marries for convenience and does not wish to compromise her easy position by infidelity.

One day the news was circulated that Tío Tòni's son was in Valencia. The war was over. The batallions, without arms, and with that sickly aspect of ailing flocks, were disembarking in the ports. They were famished specters, feverish phantoms, as yellow as candles seen in funeral ceremonies, their will-to-live sparkling in their eyes, which were as deep as a star at the bottom of a well. They all marched off to their homes, incapable of ever working again, and destined to die off within a year, in the bosom of their families, who had given a man and received in return a shadow.

Tonet was welcomed in Palmar with curiosity and enthusiasm. He was the only one from the place that had come back. And how he came back! . . . . emaciated and weakened by the privations of the final days of the war, for he was among those who had been through the blockade of Santiago. But apart from this he looked well, and the old women admired his thin, wiry figure, the military poses that he assumed at the foot of the rachitic olive that adorned the square, twirling his mustache (a manly decoration that was worn in all Palmar only by the chief of the carabineers), and exhibiting his great collection of straw hats,—the sole wardrobe he had brought back from the war. At night Cañamèl's place would be thronged with folks who were eager to hear all about the island beyond the seas.

He had forgotten his military braggadoccio, the times when he had thrashed suspected non-combatants and entered the hovels revolver in hand. Now all his tales were about the Americans,—the Yankees he had seen at Santiago; a set of tall, sinewy fellows who ate plenty of meat and wore tiny hats. And here his descriptions ended. The huge stature of the enemy was the sole impression that had remained in his memory. And the silence of the tavern was rent with loud guffaws when Tonet recounted the story of one of those chaps, who, finding him covered with rags, had presented him with a pair of trousers before he embarked for Spain,—so wide and long that they covered him almost like a sail.

Neleta, behind the bar, listened, and gazed at him fixedly. Her eyes were inexpressive; the two green drops were lustreless, but not for an instant did they leave Tonet, as if they were eager to retain the image of that martial figure, so distinct from the appearance of all who surrounded him, and so utterly different from the youth who ten years before had been her sweetheart.

Cañamèl, touched by patriotism and enthused by the extraordinary crowds that Tonet attracted to the tavern, shook hands with the soldier, offered him glass after glass, and questioned him about Cuba, learning of the changes that had taken place since that remote time when he had been there.

Tonet went everywhere, escorted by Sangonera, who was filled with admiration for his boyhood chum. He had abandoned the books loaned to him by the vicars. His father's weakness for the wandering life and wine had awakened in him, and the curate had thrown him out of church, tired of the droll stupidities he would commit while assisting him, dead drunk, at mass. Besides, Sangonera did not agree, as he remarked gravely amid the laughter of all, with the curate's way of looking at things. And aged in his youth by an interminable drunkenness, tattered and grimy, he lived from hand to mouth, as in his childhood days, sleeping in his shanty, which was worse than a pig-sty, and showing his gaunt, ascetic figure, which scarcely cast a shadow upon the floor, wherever there was a drink to be had.

In Tonet's company he found many a treat, and he was the first in the tavern to ask the soldier to tell his tales, for he knew that after the story would come the drinks.

The repatriated warrior was content with this life of ease and admiration. Palmar now seemed an abode of delight, in comparison with the memory of nights passed in the trench, his stomach collapsing with hunger, and of the terrible trip in a vessel laden with ailing flesh, strewing the sea with corpses.

After a month of this easy life, his father one night spoke to him in the silence of the cabin. What did he intend to do? Now he was a man and should consider his wild oats sown and think seriously of the future. He had certain plans of his own, which he desired to communicate to his son and only heir. By laboring unremittingly, with the persistence of honest men, they might yet make a little fortune. A city woman, the same that had rented out the Saler lands to him, won over by his sim-

plicity and his diligence, had just presented to him a large
tract of land close to the lake; a *tancat* that could produce
countless bushels of grain.

There was only one thing in the way of commencing
the proper cultivation, and this was, that the gift was
under water, and the fields would have to be filled in by
carrying many boatloads of earth,—many indeed!

That meant either spending a lot of money, or doing
it one's self. But, what the devil! They must not lose
courage. That's the way all the land around the Albufera
had been formed. The rich possessions of today had been
part of the lake fifty years previous, and two healthy,
spirited men who were not afraid of work could perform
miracles. That was far better than fishing in wretched
spots or working land owned by another.

Tonet was attracted by the novelty of the enterprise.
If they had asked him to till the best and oldest fields
near Palmar, he might have made a wry face; but the
idea of battling with the lake, of converting the water
into land that could be cultivated, of causing harvests to
arise where formerly eels wriggled among the aquatic
plants, appealed to him. Besides, in the rapidity of his
thought, he could already behold only the results, without taking the actual labor into account. They would be
wealthy and he could rent out the lands, living the life
of an idler, which was his chief ambition.

Father and son attacked the task, aided by La Borda,
who was ever inspired by anything that would add to the
prosperity of the house. As to the grandfather, nothing
might be expected of him. The project had made him
just as indignant as when his son had first decided to
devote himself to land cultivation. More fellows who

wished to cramp the lake of Albufera by converting the water into fields.

And those who were committing such an indignity were of his own family! The bandits! . . .

Tonet attacked the work with all that momentary ardor characteristic of weak-willed creatures. His desire was to fill at a single stroke that corner of the lake where his father sought riches. Even before dawn, Tonet and La Borda would go off, in two little boats, in search of earth, to bring it, after more than an hour's journey, to the wide stretch of dead water whose limits were marked by the mud banks.

The work was fatiguing, overwhelming, an ant-like task. Only Tío Tòni, with the bravery of the indefatigable toiler, was capable of having attacked it without any aid other than his family and his two arms.

They went to the large canals that flow into the Albufera; to the harbors of Catarroja and Saler. With wide forks they tore out of the bed huge lumps of mud, hunks of gelatinous peat, which stirred up a horrible stench. These lumps from the bottom of the canals they would leave to dry on the banks, and when the sun converted them into whitish clods, they would load them into the two boats, which would join and form a single vessel. After an hour's incessant poling they would have carried to the *tancat* the heap of earth they had so painfully got together, and the waters would swallow it without any apparent result, as if the cargo had dissolved without leaving a trace. The fishermen would notice the laborious family pass by two or three times during the day, gliding along like gnats over the polished surface of the lake.

Tonet soon wearied of this dredging and filling in. His will-power could not hold out; after the fascination of the first moment had evaporated, he saw how monotonous the work was, and with terror calculated the months and even the years that were needed to bring the work to completion. He thought of what it would have cost to dredge up each heap of earth, and trembled with emotion to behold how the water grew muddy as it received the cargo, and then grew clear again, showing an unaltered bed, as deep and level as ever, without the slightest hump, as if all the earth poured in had escaped through a hidden hole.

He began to shirk the labor. As a pretext he spoke of the return of certain ailments that he had caught during the war, and would remain at the cabin. No sooner would La Borda and his father leave, however, than he would run off to his new corner in Cañamèl's place, where partners were never lacking for a game of *truque,* and where the jug was always within reach. At most he worked two days a week.

Tío Paloma, in his hatred for the men who were robbing the lake by filling it in, celebrated his grandson's indolence with loud laughter. Hee! Hee! . . . . His son had been a fool to have any faith in Tonet. He knew the boy well. He had been born with a stiff spine that prevented his bending over and working. His soldiering had made it stiffer than ever, and there was no helping it now at all. He knew the only medicine: only the gallows could break him!

But since at bottom he was happy to see his son suffer difficulty in his enterprise, he accepted Tonet's laziness and even smiled to him when he met him at Cañamèl's place.

The town began to gossip about Tonet's frequent visits to the tavern. He would always sit down before the bar, and Neleta and he would look and look at each other. The proprietress spoke less to Tonet than to other customers, but during the less busy moments, when she would be sitting before the casks doing something or other, every time she raised her eyes they would gaze instinctively in the youth's direction. The customers also observed that the Cubano, after his card games, sought out Neleta with his glance.

Cañamèl's former sister-in-law carried this news from door to door. They had an understanding between themselves! All you had to do was look at them and you could see that! They were going to make a ridiculous fool out of that old tavern-keeper! Between the two of them they would eat up the whole fortune that her poor sister had amassed! And when the least credulous mentioned the impossibility of the two getting together in a tavern full of customers, the harpy protested. They would meet outside the place. Neleta was capable of anything, and he, an enemy of work, had taken up his place in the tavern, certain that he would be supported there.

Cañamèl, unaware of these rumors, treated Tonet as his best friend. He played cards with him and scolded his wife if she did not invite him. He read nothing in Neleta's glance, in the strange, slightly ironical glitter of her eyes as she received these reproofs and offered her former sweetheart a glass.

The rumors that were circulating through Palmar at last reached Tío Tòni's ears, and one night, taking his son out of the cabin, he spoke to him with the sadness of a wearied man struggling in vain against misfortune.

Tonet did not care to help him,—he saw that clearly. He was the same lazy good-for-nothing as before, born to spend his life in the tavern. Now he was a man: he had been to war, and his father could not support him as he had formerly done. Didn't he want to work? . . . . Very well; he would keep on working all by himself, even though he should die like a dog, always in the hope of leaving a bit of bread at his death to the ingrate that had deserted him.

But what he could not look upon calmly was to see his son spend all his days in Cañamèl's place, in the company of his former sweetheart. He could go to other taverns; any one at all, except that one.

Tonet protested vehemently at these words. Lies, all lies! Slander that La Samaruca had invented; that malignant beast, Cañamèl's sister-in-law, who hated Neleta and didn't care what she said! And Tonet spoke all this with the energetic accents of truth, vowing by the memory of his mother that he hadn't touched so much as a finger of Neleta's, nor said the least word that might recall their former betrothal.

Tío Tòni smiled sadly. He believed it: he didn't doubt these words at all. More: he was certain that up to now all the talk had been mere gossip. But he knew life. Now it was only glances; tomorrow, attracted by continual contact, they would, as result of this dangerous game, fall into dishonor. Neleta had always seemed to him a vain, light-headed creature, and she wasn't of the sort to give any example of prudence.

After this, the spirited laborer spoke in such sincere, kindly accents that he impressed Tonet.

He must remember that he was the son of an honest man, with bad luck in his affairs, but whom nobody in all the Albufera could reproach for an evil deed.

Neleta had a husband, and he who seeks another man's wife adds treachery to sin. Besides, Cañamèl was a friend of his; they spent the day together, playing and drinking like comrades, and to deceive a man under such circumstances would be rank cowardice deserving of a bullet in the head.

The father's tone became solemn.

Neleta was rich, his son poor, and folks might think that he was chasing after her as a means of being supported without having to work. This is what irritated him; what converted his sadness into anger.

Rather would he see his son dead than to feel shame at such a dishonor. Tonet! Boy! . . . . He must think of his family, of the Palomas, as old as Palmar itself: a family of hard workers as unfortunate as they were upright; overwhelmed with debts because of their bad luck, but incapable of treachery.

They were children of the lake, tranquil in their misery, and on undertaking their last voyage, when God should call them, they could sail to the very foot of His throne, showing the Lord, for lack of other merits, their hands covered with callouses, like the paws of a beast, but their souls clean of all crime.

IV

THE second Sunday in July was for Palmar the most important day in the year.

It was on this day that lots were drawn by the inhabitants of the town for the *redolíns,* the fishing sites on lake Albufera and its canals. It was a solemn, traditional ceremony, presided over by a delegate from La Hacienda.[1] —a mysterious woman whom nobody had ever seen, but who was spoken of with superstitious awe, seeing that she was proprietress of the lake and the interminable pine-groves of the Dehesa.

At seven in the morning the church bell had sent the whole town scurrying off to mass. The festivities in honor of the Infant Jesus, after Christmas, were solemn indeed; but after all they were nothing more than pure diversions, while in the ceremony of the lot-drawing there was at stake the year's living and even a chance to get rich if the fishing were good.

For this reason the mass on this Sunday was the one listened to with greatest devotion. The women did not have to go looking for their husbands, pushing them along to the church and forcing them to fulfil their religious duties. All the fishermen were in church, abstracted, thinking more of the lake than of the mass, and in their mind's eye they could see the lake of Albufera and its canals, and were getting ready to select the most favorable

---

[1] The Ministry of Finance.

sites if luck smiled on them with the first numbers.

The church, small, with whitewashed walls, high windows and green curtains, could not contain all the faithful on this day. The door was wide open and the public overflowed into the square, all heads uncovered in the July sun. On the altar the Infant Jesus, the town's patron, displayed his smiling countenance and his hollow skirt; the image was no more than a palm in height, but in spite of its smallness, it was able, during stormy nights, to fill the vessels of those who had won the best places with eels, and perform other no less astounding miracles talked about by the women of Palmar.

On the walls there stood out against the white background some paintings that came from old convents: huge pictures with phalanxes of condemned souls,—all red, as if they had just been cooked,—and angels in parrot-like plumages goading them along with flaming swords.

Above the font of holy water, a little placard in Gothic characters read as follows:

Si por la ley del amor no es
lícito delinquir, no se permite
escupir en las casa del Señor.[1]

Everybody in Palmar admired these verses,—the work according to Tío Paloma, of a certain vicar who dwelt there in the olden days when the boatman was yet a boy. All had practised reading it, deciphering the words during the endless masses of their existence as good Christians. But if they admired the poetry, they did not take the advice, and the fishermen, without any respect whatsoever

---

[1] If by the law of love it is unjust to do wrong, spitting in the house of the Lord is condemned.

for the "law of love," coughed and spat with their chronic amphibian hoarseness, and the ceremony would proceed amidst a continuous hawking and expectoration that dirtied the floor and drew the angry glances of the celebrant.

Never had Palmar had a vicar like *pare Miquèl*. It was said that he had been sent thither as a punishment, but his disgrace appeared to be quite to his liking. An indefatigable huntsman, no sooner would mass be over than he would put on his esparto sandals, clap his skin cap on, and followed by his dog, he would make for the Dehesa or run his little skiff through the thick reeds to shoot coots. A fellow must help himself out in a wretched position like his, he said. The pay was five *reales* a day, and he would be condemned to die of hunger, like his predecessors, if it weren't for his gun, which the forest guards tolerated, and which brought down meat for his table every day. The women admired his vigorous integrity of character, seeing that he all but regulated them with his fists. The men applauded no less the simple directness with which he went about his religious duties. He was a gun-priest. When the town magistrate had to spend the night in Valencia, he would delegate his authority to Don Miguel, and the latter, content with the change, would say to the chief of the coast-guardsmen:

"You and I are the only authorities of the town. Let's watch well over it."

And, with their guns slung across their shoulders, they would make their nocturnal rounds, entering the taverns to send the men off to bed, stopping at the presbytery several times to drink a glass of cane-liquor, until daybreak. Then Don Miguel, laying aside his weapon and his contrabandist uniform, would enter the church to say mass for the fishermen.

Sundays, while he performed the sacred rites, he would look out of the corner of his eye at the faithful, noting those who kept on spitting, the gossips who chattered about their neighbors, the youngsters pushing each other near the door; and on turning around, drawing his proud body erect for the communal blessing, he would stare so reprovingly at the guilty ones that they trembled in anticipation of *pare Miquèl's* threats. It was he who had kicked out drunken Sangonera, having caught him the third or fourth time with the wine-bottle of the sacristy. In his house only the priest could drink. His natural violence accompanied him in all his sacred functions, and many a time, in the midst of mass, noticing that the successor to Sangonera was making mistakes in the responses or was slow in fetching the Gospel from one side to the other, he would give him a kick from behind the lace trimmings of his alb, clucking his tongue as if he were calling a dog.

His morality was a simple code: it dwelt in the stomach. When the penitent parishioners excused their faults at confession, the penance imposed was always the same. What they needed was to eat more! That's why the evil spirit could grasp them so easily, seeing how thin and yellowish they were. As he put it: "More good food and less sin." And if anyone replied to this advice by pleading poverty, the priest would wax indignant, uttering a round oath. *Recordóns!* Poor, and they living in the Albufera, the best corner of the world? There was he himself with his five *reales* per day, and he had a better time of it than any patriarch. They had banished him to

Palmar thinking to give him a wretched lot, and he would exchange his post only for a canonry in Valencia. Why had God created the wood-cocks in the Dehesa, who swarmed as plentiful as flies, the rabbits, as numerous as the blades of grass, and all those birds of the lake, which rose from the brakes in dozens as soon as the reeds were stirred? Did they expect the meat to fall already plucked and spiced, right into their pots? .... What they needed was more attention to work and fear of God. They shouldn't give themselves up exclusively to fishing eels, spending hour after hour in a boat, like a woman, and eating whitish meat that reeked of mud. That's why they were such a disgusting lot of mouldy old sinners. A man with red blood in his veins,—*cordones!*—ought to get his food as he himself did .... with the gun! ....

After Easter, when all Palmar emptied its sack of sins in the confessional, the sounds of shots would multiply in the Dehesa and on the lake, and the guards would dash wildly here and there, at a loss to explain this sudden hunting craze.

The mass was ended, and the people scattered over the square. The women did not return to their cabins to prepare the mid-day meal. They remained with the men, before the schoolhouse, where the drawing took place. This was the best building in Palmar,—the only one with two stories,—a little structure that had its boys' section downstairs, and the girls' section above it. It was in the upper room that the drawing took place, and through the open windows could be seen the *alguacil*,[1] aided by Sangonera, arranging the table with the presidential chair for

---

[1] Constable.

the gentleman who was to come from Valencia, and the benches from the two schoolrooms, for the fishermen who belonged to the Society.

The oldest people of the town gathered about the twisted, almost barren olive tree,—the sole decoration of the little square. This snarled, ancient tree, torn up from the mountains to languish in a muddy soil, was the rendezvous of the people,—the spot where all the acts of their civic life took place. Beneath its branches all fishing arrangements were made, boats were traded, and eels were sold to the retail dealers of the city. When anybody found in the waters of the Albufera a lost *mornell,* a floating pole, or any other fishing instrument, he left it at the foot of the olive tree, and the people would file past it until the owner would recognize it by the special mark that each fisherman placed upon his belongings.

They all spoke of the approaching drawing with the tremulous emotion of those who confide their future to chance. Within an hour there would be decided, for each of them, poverty or abundance for an entire year. Among the groups the talk was chiefly confined to the six first sites,—the six best *redolins,*—the only ones that could make a fisherman rich, and which corresponded to the first six numbers that came out of the bag. These were the sites of *La Sequiòta,* or those near it,—the road followed by the eels during those stormy nights on which they ran to the sea, only to encounter the nets of the *redolins,* where they were held prisoner.

One recalled, in a mysterious tone, certain lucky fishermen who owned a site in *La Sequiòta,* and who, on a stormy night, when the lake of Albufera rolled with waves that revealed the muddy bed, had caught six hundred *arrobas*[1] *of fish*. Six hundred arrobas, at two *duros!*[2] . . . Their eyes burned with the fire of envy, but all spoke in a whisper, repeating the figures of the catch in a mysterious fashion, fearing lest some stranger should overhear them. For since childhood each of them had learned, with a strange feeling of solidarity, the advantage of always averring that fishing was bad, so that the Ministry of Finance (that unknown, hoggish old dame) should not afflict them with new taxes.

Tío Paloma spoke of the good old days when folks didn't multiply as rapidly as rabbits in the Dehesa, and when the drawing was entered by only some sixty fishermen who alone made up the Society. How many were they now? In the drawing of the previous year more than a hundred and fifty had participated. If the population continued to grow, the fishermen would outnumber the eels and Palmar would lose the advantages of its *redolin* privilege, which gave it a certain superiority over all the other fishing communities of the lake.

The recollection of these "others,"—of the fishermen of Catarroja who shared with those of Palmar the use of the lake, irritated Tío Paloma. He hated them as much as he hated the farmers who robbed the water in their creation of new fields. According to what the old boatman said, those fishermen who lived far from the lake, in the suburbs of Catarroja, mingling with the farmers and working the soil when pay was big, were merely occasional fishermen, persons who came to the water impelled by hunger, for lack of more productive employment.

---

[1] Arroba=a *weight* of 25 lbs., or a *measure* of 32 pints.
[2] Dollars.

The pride of these enemies rankled in Tío Paloma's soul, for they considered themselves the earliest settlers of la Albufera. According to them, the inhabitants of Catarroja were the oldest fishermen,—those to whom the glorious king, Don Jaime, after conquering Valencia, gave first privilege to exploit the lake, with the obligation of giving over to the crown the fifth part of the catch.

"What were the folk of Palmar in those days?" they would ironically ask the old boatman. And he grew indignant as he recalled the answer given by the people from Catarroja. Palmar bore its name because in ancient times it had been an islet covered with palmettos. In the early centuries people from Torrente and other places had come down, setting themselves to the broom business; they established themselves upon the island, and after gathering a supply of palmettos for the whole year, would return. Little by little a few families would remain. The broom-makers were converted into fishermen, since fishing was more profitable; and because, as a result of their wandering life, they were more clever and abreast of the world's progress, they invented the *redolins*, receiving in return for this a special privilege from the monarchs and prejudicing the interests of the folks from Catarroja,— a simple people that had never left the Albufera. . . .

It was a sight to behold, Tío Paloma's indignation when he repeated the enemy's opinions. The people of Palmar, who were the most expert fishermen of the lake, descendants of broom-makers, coming from Torrente and other places, where no eel had ever been bred! . . . . Christ! For less reason than this men slew each other on some bank, with a *fitora*. He knew all about it, and he replied that it was all an infamous lie.

When he was a young man they had named him
Warden of the Society, and he had carried off to his home
the treasure of the town,—the fishermen's archives: a
box filled with big books, ordinances, privileges from
monarchs, and accounts, which passed from one Warden
to another at each new election, and had for centuries been
knocking about from cabin to cabin, always kept under-
neath the mattress, as if the enemies of Palmar might try
to rob it. The old boatman did not know how to read.
In his day they never thought of such things, and they
had more to eat. But a certain vicar, a friend of his, had
during the nights deciphered for him the contents of those
pen-scratchings that filled the yellowish pages, and he had
easily retained them in his memory. First, the privilege
of the glorious Saint Jaime, the slayer of the Moors; for
the boatman, in his reverence for the conqueror king, who
had given the lake to the fishermen, thought royalty a
small matter and made a saint of him. Then came the
concessions of Don Pedro, Doña Violante, Don Martin,
Don Fernando,—all monarchs and some of them blessed
servants of God who remembered the poor; this one had
given them the right to cut logs in the Dehesa for the
weighting of nets, the other the privilege of using the pine
bark for dyeing the meshes,—all had conceded something
to the fishermen. Those were other times. The monarchs,
excellent persons, were content with a fifth of the annual
catch: not as now, when the Ministry of Finance and
other inventions of man carried off every three months a
half *arroba* of silver for letting them live by a lake that
had belonged to their forebears. And when anyone told
him that the fifth was equivalent to much more than the
famous half *arroba* of silver, Tío Paloma would scratch

his head under his cap, at a loss. Very well: agreed that
it was more; but it was not paid in money and it was
felt far less.

Then he would return to his mania against the other
inhabitants of the lake. It was true that at the beginning
there existed no other fishermen in the Albufera than
those who dwelt in the shadow of Catarroja's bell-tower.
In those days it was impossible to live near the sea. The
Barbary pirates were most dangerous near the shore,
sweeping everything away, and honest, hard-working people were forced to take shelter in the towns lest their
necks be adorned with a chain. But little by little, as times
grew more safe, the true fishermen, the genuine,—those
who fled the tilling of the soil as a dishonorable abdica-
tion, had moved to Palmar, thus avoiding a daily trip of
two hours before casting their nets. They loved the lake
and that's why they had remained near it. There was no
broom-making about it! The inhabitants of Palmar were
as old as the others. He had often heard from his grandfather that the family came from Catarroja, and that
there must be relatives of theirs there yet, though he did
not care to know anything of them.

The proof that they were the oldest and most expert
fishermen lay in the invention of the *redolins*: a wonderful invention that the folks of Catarroja had never been
able to fathom. Those wretches fished with nets and
hooks; most of the days they had to cross their stomachs,
and no matter how favorable conditions were, they'd never
be anything more than poor people. The folks of Palmar,
with their wisdom, had studied the habits of the eels.
Noticing that during the night they set out for the sea,
and that during the darkness of storms they dash about

like mad, abandoning the lake and making for the canals,
they had found it more to their advantage to close the
canals with barriers of sunken nets, placing beside them
the snares for *mornells* and *monòts,* and the fish, deceived, came swimming right into the nets, without any
more work for the fisherman than emptying the contrivances and lowering them anew.

And what an admirable organization was the Society
of Palmar! Tío Paloma went into ecstasies over this ar-
rangement of the old fishermen. The lake belonged to
the fisherfolk. Everything belonged to everybody; not
as on dry land, where men have invented such messes as
division of land, placing boundaries and walls, and spout-
ing with pride that "this is thine and this is mine," as if
everything wasn't God's, and as if, when they died, they
could own any more earth than that which filled their
mouths forever.

The Albufera for all the sons of Palmar, without any
class distinction; the same for the tramps that spent their
day in Cañamèl's tavern as for the chief magistrate, who
sent eels far, far off, and was almost as wealthy as the
tavern-keeper. But since, if the lake were to be appor-
tioned among them, some places were better than others,
they had established the annual drawing, and the good
morsels passed from hand to hand. He who today was
poverty-stricken might tomorrow be a rich man: thus did
the Lord ordain, through the luck of the various partici-
pants. He who was destined to be poor, would be poor,
but with a window open to let Fortune in if she felt the
whim. There was he, who was the oldest inhabitant of
Palmar, and expected to round out his century if the devil
didn't interfere. He had taken part in more than eighty

drawings; once he drew fifth place, once the fourth; he had never drawn first, but he had no complaint to offer, for he had lived without suffering hunger and without wracking his brains for some way to cheat his neighbor, like the folks who came from the inland towns. Besides, when winter was over, and when the large catches in the *redolíns* were finished, the Warden ordered an *arrastrá*, in which all the fishermen of the Society participated, pooling their nets, their boats and their arms. And this community enterprise, involving an entire town, swept the bottom of the lake with its gigantic mesh of nets, and the product of the huge catch was divided among all the men equally. That was the way men should live, like brothers, lest they be transformed into beasts. And Tío Paloma would finish by saying that it was not without significance that the Lord, when he came upon the earth, preached in lakes that were, more or less, like the Albufera, and did not surround himself with land cultivators, but rather with tench and eel fisheries.

The crowd in the square grew greater and greater. The chief magistrate, with his assistants and the *alguacil,* was in the canal awaiting the vessel that was to bring the representative of the Ministry of Finance from Valencia. The folks from the surrounding country arrived to sanctify the drawing with their presence. The crowd made way for the lieutenant of the carabineers, who came from his solitude at Torre Nueva, between the Dehesa and the sea, on his galloping horse, bespattered with the mud of the canals. He presented himself to the Warden, followed by a sinewy youth who carried on his back the box of the Society's archives. *Pare Miquèl,* the bellicose vicar, with his cassock on his shoulder and his cap askew, was going from group to group assuring everybody that luck would turn its back upon the fishermen.

Cañamèl, who was not a native of the town, and therefore had no right to take part in the drawing, was nevertheless as deeply interested as the fishermen. He never missed that ceremony. It was there, indeed, that he found his business for the whole year, which compensated for the decline of his smuggling interests. Almost always he who won the first choice was a poor fellow, with no other property than a skiff and a few nets. In order to exploit La Sequiòta considerable equipment was required, as well as several boats and hired sailors; and when the humble chap, overwhelmed by his good fortune, was at a loss how to go about things, Cañamèl would approach him like a good angel. He had the necessary means; he offered his boats, the thousand *pesetas'* worth of new twine for the large barrier nets that were needed to close the canal, and the money necessary for advancing pay. All as assistance to a friend, on account of the affection that the man inspired in him. But as friendship is one thing and business another, he would be content with half of the profits from the catch in return for his aid. In this manner the drawings usually worked to Cañamèl's benefit; he awaited the outcome anxiously, praying that the best choices should not fall to those of Palmar who had money.

Neleta, too, had come to the square, attracted by the proceedings, which furnished one of the liveliest of the town holidays. She came in her best clothes, and looked like a lady from Valencia; La Samaruca, her terrible enemy, stood in the middle of a group, poking fun at her high chignon, her rose-colored suit, her belt with its silver buckle, and her general impression of a "bad woman," which scandalized all Palmar, turning the men's heads. Ever since she had become wealthy the attractive blonde had perfumed herself in most violent fashion, as if she were intent upon liberating herself from the stench of mire that enwrapped the lake. She washed her face very seldom, like all the women of the island; her skin was not clean, but it never lacked a layer of powder, and at every step her clothes scattered an overpowering odor of musk, which sent whiffs of voluptuous blessedness through the dilating nostrils of the tavern customers.

There was a great stir amid the crowd. He was already there! . . . . The ceremony was about to begin. And before the multitude passed the *alcalde* with his black-tasseled cane, all his assistants and the delegate from the Ministry of Finance,—a poor employé who was stared at in admiration by all the fishermen (who in confused fashion attributed to him such a power over the Albufera) and at the same time with intense hatred. That was the dandy who swallowed up the half *arroba* of silver!

All slowly climbed the narrow little school staircase, whose width could accommodate but a single person at a time. A couple of carabineers, gun in hand, stood guard at the door so as to prevent the entrance of the women and children, who disturbed the deliberations of the meeting. From time to time the curiosity of the youngsters would make them try to fool the guards, but the carabineers would bring the butt-ends of their guns into play and threaten to thrash the entire gang, which with its hullabaloo was interfering with the solemnity of the drawing.

Above, the assembly was so dense that the fishermen, not being able to find a seat upon the benches, crowded about the balconies. Some, the oldest of them, wore the

red cap of the inhabitants of the Albufera; others covered
their heads with the wide-bordered handkerchiefs of the
farmer folk, or with palm hats. All were dressed in
bright colors, with esparto sandals or barefoot altogether,
and from this sweating, packed assembly rose the eternal,
viscous, cold stench of amphibians brought up in mud.

On the teacher's platform was the presidential desk. In
the center was the envoy from Valencia, dictating to his
secretary the opening phrases of the record of proceedings, and at his side the priest, the chief magistrate, the
Warden, the lieutenant and other invited guests, among
whom figured the physician of Palmar, a poor pariah of
the profession, who for five *reales* came sailing three
times weekly to cure en masse the wretched sufferers from
the tertian fever.

The Warden rose from his seat. Before him lay the
account books of the Society,—marvellous hieroglyphics,
in which not a single word was written, since the pay-
ments were recorded by all manner of symbols. Thus
had the ancient Wardens done, who had not known how
to write, and thus was the accounting continued. Each
page contained the account of a fisherman. There was
no inscription of his name at the top, but only the mark
that each one placed upon his skiff and his nets, for purposes of identification. One was a cross, the other a pair
of shears, the next a coot's bill, Tío Paloma a crescent,
and the Warden understood them all, having only to
glance at the hieroglyphics to say: "This is So-and-so's account." And on the rest of the page, lines and more lines,
each stroke signifying the payment of a month's dues.

The old boatman praised this system of accounting. In
this manner everyone could look over his own accounts,

and there were no tricks such as filled those huge tomes
of figures and fine handwriting, which were understood
only by educated gentlemen.

The Warden, a lively youth with a shaven head and
insolent eyes, coughed and spat out several times before
speaking. The invited guests, who occupied the platform,
leaned back and began to converse among themselves.
First the Society affairs were to be discussed, and they
could take no part. Those were matters that must be
settled among fishermen. The Warden began his speech:
"Caballers! . . . ."

And he passed his imperious glance over the crowd, imposing silence. Below, in the square, the children were
yelling like the damned, and the conversation of the
women rose to the hall with a bothersome humming.
The chief magistrate sent the *alguacil* out among the
folk to quiet them, so that the Warden might continue
his speech.

Gentlemen,—plain talk. He had been elected Warden
to collect from each one his dues and send every three
months to the Treasury about one thousand five hundred
pesetas, the much-talked of half *arroba* of silver. Very
well; things could not go on as they were going. Many
were in arrears, and the fishermen best off had to supply
that deficit. In order to avoid all this disorder in the
future, he proposed that all who were not paid up on the
books should be excluded from the drawing.

Part of the public received this suggestion with murmurs of approval. These were the ones who had paid up,
and if many of their companions should be excluded from
the drawing, their own chances of drawing an early choice
would rise. But the majority of the members,—those

who looked most wretched,—protested at the top of their
lungs, jumping to their feet in their excitement. It was
several minutes before the Warden could make himself
heard.

When silence was re-established there arose a sickly
man, with a pale face and an unhealthy glint in his eyes.
He spoke slowly, in a feeble voice; his words were every
now and then cut short by feverish shivering. He was of
those who had not paid: perhaps nobody was so much
behind as he. In the drawing of the year before he had
got one of the last places and he hadn't caught enough to
feed his family. In one year he had sailed twice toward
Valencia, bearing in the bottom of the boat two white
caskets adorned with gold fringe, two trips that had
forced him to borrow money. . . . But—ay!—what less
can a father do but dress his little ones in the best when
they go off on their last journey! . . . . Two little children
had died on his hands from not eating enough,—eating
ill, as *pare Miquèl,* there present, put it, and afterward he
had caught the tertian fever while at work, and this had
put him months and months behind. He had not paid because he simply could not. And were they, for this reason, to deprive him of his chance to win a fortune? Did
he not belong to the Society of Fishermen, as his father
and grandfather before him had done? . . . .

There was a painful silence, amid which could be heard
the sobbing of the unhappy fellow, who had fallen exhausted into his seat, his head in his hands, as if ashamed
of his confession.

"*No, redeu, no!* No, by God, no!" shouted a trembling
voice with a passionate energy that stirred everybody.

It was Tío Paloma who, having jumped to his feet, his

cap shoved tightly down over his head, his eyes flaming with indignation, began to speak post haste, mingling with every other word all the oaths and the curses that were stored in his memory. His old companions pulled his sash to remind him that he must show some respect for the gentlemen on the platform; but he replied with a thrust of his elbow and continued. Much he cared about those puppets,—he, a man who had dealt with heroes and monarchs! . . . . He spoke because he *could* speak. Christ! He was the oldest boatmen of the Albufera, and his words should be taken like gospel. The fathers and grandfathers of all present spoke through his mouth. La Albufera belonged to all,—didn't it?—and it was an outrage to deprive a man of his bread just because he had or hadn't paid the Treasury. Did that lady need the miserable *pesetas* of a poor fisherman to buy her supper with? . . . .

The indignation of the old man was communicated to the public. Many were laughing loudly, forgetting the painful impression of the moment previous.

Tío Paloma recalled that he, too, had been Warden. It was all very well to be harsh toward those wretches who flee from hard work; but as for the poor fellows who do their duty and who can't pay because they are the victims of poverty,—one should open his hands to them. *Cordones!* Were the fishermen of Palmar a band of Moors? No; they were all brothers, and the lake belonged to all. This division of rich and poor was good enough for dry land, for the *labradores,* among whom there are masters and serfs. In the Albufera all were equal: he who did not pay now would pay later; and let those who had more supply the deficit of those who had nothing, for it

had always been that way. . . . Let everybody participate
in the drawing!

Tonet gave the signal for the thunderous applause that
acclaimed his grandfather. Tío Tòni did not seem to be
in full accord with his father's notions, but all the poor
fishermen rushed upon the old man, demonstrating their
enthusiasm by pulling at his smock and giving him such
vehement, hearty, affectionate slaps across the back that
they fell upon his wrinkled neck like a shower of blows.

The Warden closed the books with an expression of
discouragement. It was the same story every year. With
these old folk, who seemed ever young, it was impossible
to put the Society's affairs in order. And with a bored
air he listened to the excuses offered for not having paid
the dues or for having delayed the payment. There were
sick persons in the family; they had drawn a bad site;
the cursed fever had rendered them unfit to work,—the
cursed fever which seemed at night to spy upon them from
behind the canebrakes that it might fasten its claws into
the flesh of the poor; and all the misery, the sad existence
of the unhealthful lagoon went filing by like an endless
lamentation.

In order to cut short this infinite exposition of sorrows
it was agreed upon to exclude none from the drawing,
and the Warden deposited upon the table the skin sack
and the labels.

"Demane la paraula! I want to speak!" shouted a
voice near the entrance.

Who was it wished to begin the speaking all over again,
and all the boresome claims? The groups opened and an
outburst of laughter greeted the appearance of Sangonera,

who advanced gravely, rubbing his rheumy, drunkard's eyes and making every effort to look dignified enough to take part in the meeting. Having found all the taverns of Palmar deserted, he had made his way into the school-house and thought it necessary to ask for the floor before the drawing began.

"*Que vòls tu?* What do you wish?" asked the Warden ill-humoredly, vexed by this intrusion of the tramp, which, coming on the heels of the debtors' recital of excuses, utterly exhausted his patience.

What did he wish? . . . . He wished to know why his name did not figure in the annual drawings? He had as much right as any other to enjoy a *redolí* in the Albufera. He was the poorest of them all; but had he not been born in Palmar? Hadn't he been baptized in the parish of San Valero, in Ruzafa? Was he not a descendant of fishermen? Then he ought to participate in the drawing.

And the claims of this loafer, who had never cared to touch a net and preferred swimming across the canals to touching a pole with his hand seemed so unheard-of, so grotesque to the fishermen, that they all burst into guffaws.

The Warden answered in a provoked manner. Out of the place, *maltrabaja!* What did the Society care whether his forbears had been honest fishermen, when his father had abandoned the boatman's pole in order to give himself up entirely to idleness, and when the only boatman qualities he could show was that of his having been born in Palmar? Besides, his father had never paid his dues, nor had he; the mark which in former days was used by the Sangoneras on their fishing instruments had many years ago been scratched off the books of the Society.

But the drunkard insisted, alleging his rights amid the rising laughter of the public, until Tío Paloma intervened with his questions. . . . And suppose he were admitted to the drawing, and he got one of the best sites, what would he do with it? How would he work it, if he were not a fisherman and knew nothing about the calling?

The vagabond smiled maliciously. The important thing was to draw the site; the rest he would see to. He would arrange matters so that others should do the work for him, giving him the greater part of the profits. And in his cynical smile vibrated the malignant expression of the first man who deceived his fellow being, making him work so that he himself might live a life of idleness.

Sangonera's frank confession incensed the fishermen. He had really done no more than formulate aloud the silent thought of many, but this simple folk felt itself insulted by the vagabond's cynicism, and thought it saw in him the personification of all those who oppress their poverty. Out with him! Out! Shoved and pinched, he was shown the door, while the young fishermen stamped on the floor and amid general laughter imitated a cat-and-dog fight.

The vicar, Don Miguel, arose in indignation, thrusting forward his gladiator's body, his face congested with anger. What was this? What insolence did they permit themselves before these grave, important personages who presided on the platform? . . . . He'd jump right down from the platform and break some fellow's head! . . . .

As silence at once responded to his threat, the priest sat down, content with his power, and whispered to the lieutenant:

"Do you see? Nobody understands this herd better

than I. You've got to show them the stick from time to
time."

More even than *pare Miquèl's* threats, what had established calm was the sight of the Warden handing over to
the president the list of the fishermen of the Society, so as
to ascertain that all were present.

As many men of Palmar as followed the fishing trade
were there. It was enough to be an adult, although one
still lived with his father, to figure in the drawing of the
redolíns.

The president read off the names of the fishermen,
each of whom answered: "Ave María Purísima" with a
certain unction, because of the vicar's presence. Some,
the enemies of Father Miguel, answered *"Avant!"*
(Here!) enjoying the wry face that the vicar made.

The Warden emptied a sack of grimy leather, almost as
old as the Society itself, and the balls rolled upon the
tables,—a collection of hollow wooden balls, into which
was introduced a piece of paper with the name of the
participant.

One after the other the fishermen were called to the
desk to receive their ball and a strip of paper on which
the name of the man had been written, in case he himself
could not write.

It was a sight to behold the precautions which a sus-
picious cunning forced these poor folks to adopt. The
most ignorant of the fishermen went to those who knew
how to read to see if it were really their name that was
written upon the strip of paper, and only after numerous
consultations were they convinced. Moreover, the custom of always being designated by their nicknames caused
them to experience a certain hesitancy. Their true names

were employed only on a day such as this, and they wavered, as if uncertain as to whether the names were really theirs.

Then came the greatest precautions of all. Each one hid himself by turning his face to the wall, and as he introduced the slip bearing his name into the hollow ball, he wrapped about it a wisp of straw, placed with it a match, —something that should serve as a means of identification so that his ball should not be changed. Their suspicion accompanied them until the moment in which they deposited the ball into the sack. That fellow who came from Valencia awoke in them the mistrust which a public official always inspires in rural folk.

The drawing was about to begin. The vicar, Don Miguel arose, removed his hat, and all followed his action. They were to pray a *salve*,[1] according to the old tradition; this brought good luck. And for a long time the fishermen, with their caps in their hands and their heads bowed, mumbled the prayer softly.

Absolute silence. The president stirred the leather bag to mix the balls well, and as they struck against each other in the silence, they sounded like a distant hailstorm. A little boy came up the room, passed from one to another over the fishermen's heads, and placed his hand into the sack. The anxiety was intense; all eyes were fixed upon the wooden ball, out of which was painfully being unfolded the slip of paper.

The president read the name, and a certain indecision was to be noted in the assembly, which was accustomed to nicknames and slow to recognize regular names, which were rarely used. Who had won the first

---

[1] A salutation or prayer to the Virgin.

choice? But Tonet had risen from his seat with a bound, shouting: "Present! . . . ." It was Tío Paloma's grandson! What luck the boy had! . . . . He had won first place in the very first drawing in which he had taken part!

His nearest neighbors congratulated him enviously, but he, with the anxiety of one who does not yet believe in his good fortune, looked only at the president. . . . Might he now name his choice of a fishing site? No sooner had he been answered with an affirmative nod than he named his request: he desired La Sequiòta. And when he saw the clerk write down his choice, he dashed forth like a lightning flash from the place, thrusting everybody aside and pushing away the friendly hands that were stretched out to felicitate him.

Down on the square the crowd was waiting in as intense a silence as that which reigned upstairs. It was the custom for the first winners to jump down at once and spread news of their good luck, waving their hats aloft as a sign of joy. Wherefore, as soon as they caught sight of Tonet come almost rolling down the stairs, they greeted him with loud acclamation.

"It's the Cuban! . . . . It's Tonet with the mustache! *Te el ú! Te el ú! . . . .*"

The women threw themselves upon him with vehemence of emotion, embracing him, weeping, as if they might catch some of his good luck, and recalling his mother. How glad the poor woman would be if she could only see him now! And Tonet, enwrapped in all these skirts, impelled and emboldened by the caressing ovation, instinctively embraced Neleta, who smiled, while her green eyes glittered with contentment.

The Cubano wished to celebrate his triumph. He sent

to Cañamèl's for cases of lemonade and beer for all these women. Let the men drink all they pleased. He was footing the bill! In an instant the square was converted into an encampment. Sangonera, whose activity always stirred at the mention of drink, had seconded the desires of his generous friend, fetching all the old, hard pastry that had long been stored behind the glass show-cases; and he passed from group to group, filling glasses and frequently pausing in his distribution to attend to his own wants.

The winners of the next best locations were now coming down, throwing their hats into the air and shouting *Vítol! Vítol!*[1] But only their family and their friends grouped about them. All the attention was for Tonet, for number one, who had given the people such a liberal spread.

The fishermen left the schoolhouse. Already some thirty balls had been drawn; there remained now only the bad *redolíns,*—those which gave hardly enough to eat, and the spectators left the place, no longer feeling any interest in the drawing.

Tío Paloma was going from group to group receiving congratulations. For the first time he exhibited satisfaction with his grandson. Hee, hee! . . . Luck always favors rascals; his father had said so before him. There was he with his participation in eighty drawings, and he had never drawn first place, while his grandson, just returned from wandering in distant lands, took part for the first time and drew the grand prize. But after all . . . . it was all in the family. And he glowed with the realization

---

[1] Hurrah!

that for the coming year he would be the first fisherman in Albufera.

Rendered more affectionate than usual by the good luck, he approached his son, who was as solemn and engrossed as ever. Tono! Good fortune had entered the cabin and it must be taken advantage of! He would help out the young fellow, who didn't know much about fishing, and they'd do an enormous business.

But the aged grandfather was stupefied at the coldness with which his son answered him. Yes; that first place was a bit of good luck, all right, if a man had the tools necessary for its exploitation. They needed more than a thousand *pesetas* for the nets alone. Did they have that much money? . . . .

Tío Paloma smiled. They'd easily find some one to lend it to them. But Tòni, hearing the mention of loans, made a wry face. They owed enough as it was. He suffered not a little from certain Frenchmen established in Catarroja, who sold horses on the instalment plan and advanced money to farmers. He had been forced to seek their aid, first during the years of bad harvests, and now to advance the filling-in of his lake somewhat; even in his dreams he could see those men, garbed in corduroy, jabbering threats and every moment pulling out their terrible account-book, in which they wrote down the debts with their complicated net of interest. He had enough already. When a man finds himself sunk in one bad piece of business, he should save himself as best he could, without seeking another. He had enough with his agricultural debts, and didn't care to involve himself in debts for fishing purposes. His sole desire was to bring his lands to the level of the water, without becoming further involved.

The boatman turned his shoulder upon his son. And was that creature of his flesh and blood? . . . . He preferred Tonet, with all his indolence. He would get together with his grandson and they would both manage somehow or other to solve the difficulty. The owner of *La Sequiòta* never lacked finances.

Tonet, surrounded by friends, acclaimed by the women, filled with pride because of the passionate glance that Neleta fixed upon him, felt somebody touch him upon the shoulder.

It was Cañamèl, who seemed to envelop him with his affectionate eyes. They must talk something over; not for nothing had they always been such good friends, and the tavern been practically Tonet's second home. There was no need of leaving this for later: business between friends was easily arranged. And they withdrew a few paces, followed by the curious glances of the crowd.

The tavern-keeper went straight to the point. Tonet would not have enough money with which to exploit the site he had won in the drawing. Wasn't that so? . . . . Well, then, here was he, a true friend, ready to help him out, to go into partnership with him. He would give him all he needed.

And as Tonet was silent, not knowing what to reply, the tavern-keeper, interpreting his silence as a refusal, attacked the proposition once more. Were they, or were they not, comrades? Was he thinking of doing as his father had done,—going to those foreigners at Catarroja who sucked the very blood of the poor? He was a friend; he even considered himself in a way a relative, for— what the deuce!—he could not forget that his wife, his

Neleta, had been brought up in the Palomas' cabin,—that many a time they had given her food there, and that she was as fond of Tonet as of a brother.

The greedy tavern-keeper used these recollections with the greatest cunning, insisting upon the fraternal affection that his wife felt for the young man.

Then he had recourse to more heroic methods. If he had any doubts about him, if he did not wish him as an associate in the business, he would call Neleta to convince him. Surely she would succeed in setting him upon the right road. What did he say? . . . . Should he call her?

Tonet, seduced by these proposals, hesitated before accepting. He feared the gossip of the people, and recalled his father's severe advice. He looked about him, as if he might receive an inspiration from the looks of the people, and saw his grandfather, who from a distance was nodding affirmatively to him.

The boatman had guessed what Cañamèl was saying. And he had hit precisely upon the wealthy tavern-keeper as an aid. He encouraged his grandson with renewed gestures. He must not refuse: that was the man they needed.

Tonet reached a decision, and Neleta's husband, guessing his decision from the light in his eyes, hastened to formulate the conditions. He would provide all the necessary investment, and Tonet and his grandfather would do the work. Agreed? . . . .

Agreed. The two men shook hands, and followed by Neleta and Tío Paloma walked toward the tavern to solemnize the contract at a joint meal.

At once the news went circulating about the square.

The Cubano and Cañamèl had joined forces to exploit La Sequiòta!

La Samaruca had to be removed from the square by order of the magistrate. Escorted by several women she went off in the direction of her cabin, roaring like one possessed, calling at the top of her lungs to her sister, who had died years before, shouting vociferously that Cañamèl was a shameless wretch, and that for the sake of driving a good bargain he had not hesitated to introduce into his house his own wife's lover.

V.

TONET'S position in Cañamèl's establishment
changed completely. No longer was he a mere customer. He was the partner, the companion of the place's
proprietor, and entered the tavern whenever he pleased,
defying with proud attitude the gossip of Neleta's enemies.

If he spent entire days there, it was for the purpose
of discussing business. He entered most confidently the
inner rooms, and to show that he was as much at home
as in his own house, he would get behind the counter and
sit down at Cañamèl's side. Many a time, if he and his
wife went within, and some customer should ask for
something, Tonet would leap to the bar and with comic
gravity, amid the laughter of his friends, serve the various articles, imitating the voice and the mannerisms of
Tío Paco.

The tavern-keeper was well content with his associate.
An excellent youth, as he declared before the tavern
gathering when Tonet was not present; a good friend,
who, if he would only act right and stick to business,
would go far, very far, seeing that he could count upon
the aid of so powerful a patron as the speaker.

Tío Paloma, too, frequented the tavern more than before. The family, after stormy scenes at night in the
solitude of the cabin, had divided into two factions. Tío
Tòni and La Borda went off to their fields every morning to continue their battle against the lake, trying to sink

it beneath the mounds of earth they brought so painfully from far away. Tonet and his grandfather went to Cañamèl's house to talk about their joint enterprise, soon to start.

In truth, the only ones who discussed the business were the tavern-keeper and Tío Paloma. Cañamèl praised himself, lauding the generosity with which he had accepted the partnership. He was exposing his capital without any foreknowledge of the year's catch, and was making this sacrifice content with but half of the proceeds. He was not like the foreign money-lenders of the mainland, who gave money only on excellent security and usurious interest. And all his hatred against the intruders, the ferocious rivalry in the exploitation of one's neighbors, vibrated in his words. Who were those people who little by little were getting the country into their clutches? Frenchmen who had come to Valencian territory in torn shoes and an old corduroy suit sticking to their skin. People from some province of France whose name he couldn't recall, but who had become more or less the *gallegos* of their country. Even the money that they loaned out was not their own. In France, capital produced very little interest, and these *gabachos* got it from their own country at two or three per cent to lend it to the Valencians at fifteen to twenty, thus realizing an excellent profit. Moreover, they bought horses on the other side of the Pyrenees, perhaps smuggling them across the border, and sold them on the instalment plan to the farmers, arranging the sale in such a manner that the purchaser never acquired complete ownership of the animal. There was one poor fellow who had paid as much for a worn-out old nag as if it had been the very horse of Saint James. Robbery, Tío

Paloma; robbery unworthy of Christians! And Cañamèl, speaking of these matters, would grow furious, with all the indignation and the secret envy of the usurer who is too cowardly to employ the methods of his competitors.

The boatman approved his words. That's why he preferred to have his family devoted to fishing, and that's why he grew angry to see his son contracting debts and more debts, in his absurd insistence upon being an agriculturalist. The poor farmers were nothing but slaves; all the year long they worked themselves bare to the bone, and to whom did all the profit go? It was the foreigners who carried off all the harvests: the Frenchman who loaned them the money and the Englishman who sold them the fertilizer on credit. . . . The idea of living a life of unremitting toil in order to support foreigners! No, while there were eels in the lake, let the lands be quietly covered with reeds and bulrushes, in the certainty that he would not be the one to break them up.

While the boatman and Cañamèl would converse, Tonet and Neleta, seated behind the counter, would gaze quietly at each other. The customers had become accustomed to seeing them hours and hours thus, exchanging glances as if they could devour each other; with an expression upon their countenances that did not correspond to their words, which were often of no significance. The gossipy old women who came for oil or wine remained motionless before them, with lowered glance and a silly look upon their faces, waiting till the very last drops came through the funnel into the bottle, while they cocked their ears to catch some word of the conversation; but the youth and the woman defied this espionage and continued speaking, as if they were in a deserted spot.

Tío Paloma, alarmed by such intimacy, spoke seriously
to his grandson. But could it really be that there was
something between them, as La Samaruca and other evil
tongues of the town maintained? Beware, Tonet! In
addition to being unworthy of his family, it would mean
the ruin of their business! But the grandson, with the
firmness of one who speaks the truth, struck his chest
and protested, so that the grandfather was convinced, although he felt a certain presentiment that such a friendship would have a bad end.

The narrow space behind the counter was for Tonet a
paradise. He would recall with Neleta their childhood
days; he would tell her his adventures yonder across the
seas, and when they were silent, he would feel a sweet intoxication (the same as on that night in which they had
been lost in the forest, only more intense, more ardent)
at the proximity of that body whose warmth seemed to
caress him through the clothes.

At night, after supping with Cañamèl and his wife,
Tonet would take out of his cabin an accordeon,—the
only thing he had brought along with him from Cuba besides the straw hats,—and would entertain everybody in
the tavern with the languid *habaneras* that he made the
instrument whine. He would sing *guajiras* of a sweet,
sentimental poesy, in which there was frequent reference
to zephyrs, harps and hearts as tender as the guayaba;
and the mellifluous Cuban accent in which he sang the
songs made Neleta close her eyes dreamily, throwing back
her body that she might relieve the pain in her bosom,
trembling with restrained emotion.

On the day following these serenades Neleta, with

moistened eyes, would follow Tonet all about the tavern from group to group.

The Cubano guessed what was going on within her. She had dreamed of him, hadn't she? The same thing had happened to Tonet in his cabin. All night long, stretching out his hands as if he were about to grasp her, he could see her in the darkness. And after this mutual confession they would remain quiet; certain of a moral possession which they could not exactly have explained; certain that at last they must of necessity belong to each other, however many obstacles might arise between them.

Within the town they could think of no other intimacy than the tavern conversations. All Palmar surrounded them during the day, and Cañamèl, sick and complaining, never left the house. Sometimes, moved by a passing flash of activity, the tavern-keeper would whistle to *Centella,* an old dog with a huge head, famous throughout the lake region for his remarkable sense of smell, and placing him in the boat would go out to the nearest islets of sedge to shoot coots. But after a few hours he would return coughing, complaining of the dampness, with his legs swollen like those of an elephant, as he said; he would get into a corner and not stop groaning until Neleta made him sip some glasses of hot liquids, tying several kerchiefs about his head and his neck. Neleta's eyes would glance toward the Cubano with an expression that clearly showed the scorn she felt for her husband.

The summer was coming to a close and serious thought must be given to preparations for the fishing. Before their houses the owners of the other *redolins* were arranging the large nets for the barring of the canals. Tío

Paloma was impatient. The contrivances that Cañamèl had,—which had been left over from his previous association with other fishermen,—were not enough for La Sequiòta. They needed to purchase a great deal of twine, and give employment to many women who make nets, if they were going to exploit the *redolí* adequately.

One night Tonet and his grandfather were having supper in the tavern and talking their business over seriously. They must buy better twine,—the kind that was made on the beach of Cabanal for the sea fishermen. Tío Paloma would go to buy it, as he was an expert, but the tavern-keeper would accompany him, as he wished to pay for the material directly, fearing that he might be cheated if he gave the money to the old boatman. Afterward, during the beatitude of digestion, Cañamèl began to feel terrified at the prospect of the next day's trip. He would have to rise at dawn, plunging from a warm bed into the cold mist; then he would have to cross the lake, go by land to Valencia, thence to Cabanal, and afterwards, make the whole journey back again. His massive body, flabby from inactivity, shuddered at thought of the trip. This man, who had spent a large part of his life wandering over the world, had taken such deep root in the mud of Palmar, that he grew excited at thought of a day's activity.

The desire for ease made him modify his proposal. He would remain in charge of the establishment and Neleta would accompany Tío Paloma. There was nobody like the women when it came to chaffering and getting things at the right price.

On the following morning the boatman and the tavern-keeper's wife started out on their trip. Tonet was to

He had seen Tonet from his place and had called him, without abandoning his magnificent posture. His body had fitted perfectly into the straw, and he didn't care to lose the impress of the position. . . . Afterwards he explained why he was there. He had eaten in the tavern with some carters,—excellent chaps,—who had given him a few crumbs, passing him the mug at each bite and laughing at his pleasantries. But no sooner had the customers left than the tavern-keeper, like all those of his class, showed him the door, knowing that he would order nothing on his own account. And there he was, killing time, which is man's enemy. . . . Were they friends or not? Would he invite him to a drink?

Tonet's affirmative nod overcame the tramp's laziness, and though with a certain pain, he decided to get up on his feet. They had a drink in the tavern, and then, slowly, they walked to a place on a bank that was shielded from the harbor by black boards.

Tonet had not seen Sangonera for many days, and the vagabond recounted his troubles.

There was nothing for him to do in Palmar. Neleta, Cañamèl's wife, was a haughty woman altogether too forgetful of her origin; she had sent him away from the tavern on the pretext that he dirtied the chairs and the tiles of the wainscoating with the mud from his clothes. In the other taverns things were wretched indeed: all poverty-stricken, and never a drinker came that could treat a fellow; so that he had been forced to quit Palmar, to wander about the lake towns, as his father had done of old; to go from place to place, ever in quest of generous friends.

Tonet, whose laziness had so disgusted his own family,

had the effrontery to offer advice. Why didn't he go to work?. . . .

Sangonera made a gesture of stupefaction. He, too! . . . . The Cubano, too, allowed himself to repeat the same advice as the old folks of Palmar! Did he himself care so much for work? Why wasn't he with his father, then, filling in the fields, instead of idling the day away at Cañamèl's, at Neleta's side, sitting back at his ease like a gentleman and drinking of the best? . . .

The Cubano smiled, not knowing what to answer and he admired the logic of the drunkard in his rejection of the advice.

The tramp seemed to have been softened by the glass that Tonet had paid for. The calm of the harbor, interrupted by the hammering of the calkers and the clucking of the hens, excited his loquacity, impelling him to impart confidences.

No, Tonet, he could not work; he would never work, even though they tried to compel him. Toil was the invention of the devil: a disobedience of God; the most serious of sins. Only corrupt souls, those who could not adapt themselves to their poverty, those who lived tormented by the desire of hoarding, even if it were poverty, thinking forever of the morrow, could give themselves up to work, converting themselves from men into beasts. He had given much thought to the matter; he knew far more than the Cubano imagined, and he didn't wish to lose his soul by devoting himself to regular, monotonous labor in order to have a house and a family and assure himself bread for the following day. That was to doubt the mercy of God, who never abandons His creatures; and he was above all a Christian.

Tonet laughed to hear these words, considering them the rambling chatter of intoxication, and nudged his tattered companion. If he expected another glass for all this nonsense, he was mistaken! What he thought was that the tramp hated work. The same held true of the others, but in varying degree; everybody bent his back, although it might be most unwillingly.

Sangonera let his gaze wander across the surface of the canal, which was tinted purple by the waning light of the afternoon. His thoughts seemed to wing far away: he spoke slowly, with a certain mysticism that contrasted with his alcoholic breath.

Tonet was an ignoramus, like everybody else in Palmar. This he declared, with the courage of intoxication, without any fear that his friend, who was quick-tempered, would give him such a shove that he'd go rolling into the canal. Hadn't he just said that all bent their backs unwillingly? And what did this prove but that work is something contrary to nature and to the dignity of man? . . . . He knew more than folks in Palmar gave him credit for: more than many of the vicars whom he had served like a slave. That's why he had always wrangled with them. He possessed the truth, and he could not dwell with the blind in spirit. While Tonet had been wandering in those lands across the sea, mixed up in battles, he had been reading the priests' books and passing the afternoons at the door of the presbytery, reflecting upon the open pages, amid the silence of a town whose populace had fled to the lake. He had committed to memory almost all the New Testament, and he seemed to tremble as he recalled reading the Sermon on the Mount for the first time. It seemed to him then that

a cloud had been rent before his very eyes. All at once
he had understood why his will rebelled before stultifying,
painful labor. It was the flesh, it was sin that made
men live in the degradation of beasts, for the satisfaction
of their earthly appetites. The soul protested against
such servitude, saying to man: "Toil not," and the sweet
intoxication of indolence was diffused through his limbs,
like a foretaste of that felicity which awaits the good
in heaven.

"Ascolta, Tonet, ascolta. Listen, Tonet, listen to me,"
said Sangonera to his friend in solemn accents.

And he recalled in disordered fashion all his evangelical readings; the precepts that had remained imprinted in
his memory. He did not have to ask anxiously for food
and clothing, for, as Jesus had said, the birds of the air
neither sow nor reap, yet despite this, they eat; nor do
the lilies of the field need to spin for their clothes, for
they are clothed by the grace of the Lord. He was a
creature of God and entrusted himself into His hands.
He did not wish to insult the Lord by working, as if he
doubted that the divine bounty would aid him. Only
the heathens, or what amounted to the same thing, the
folk of Palmar, who hoarded all the money they made
in fishing without ever inviting a fellow to drink, were
capable of toiling away for the sole purpose of laying
aside, ever doubtful of the morrow.

He wished to be like the birds of the lake, like the
flowers that grew in the reed-grass,—free, idle, and
with no other recourse than divine Providence. In his
poverty he never doubted the morrow. "Sufficient unto
the day is the evil thereof." The coming day would bring
its ills. For the moment he was content with the bit-

terness of the present: poverty, which gave him his intention to maintain himself pure, without the slightest stain of work or of earthly ambition in a world where everybody fought his neighbors in the struggle for existence, each one injuring and sacrificing his fellow-man in order to rob him of a little comfort.

Tonet listened laughingly to the words of the drunkard, uttered with a growing exaltation. He banteringly expressed admiration of his ideas and suggested that he leave the lake and enter a monastery, where he would not have to battle against poverty. But Sangonera protested indignantly.

He had quarrelled with the vicar, leaving the presbytery forever, because he could not endure beholding in his former friends a spirit utterly contrary to that of the books they read. They were like the others: they lived consumed by the desire for the other fellow's *peseta,* thinking only of food and clothing, and complaining of the decline of piety when no money came into the house, worrying every morning, doubting the bounty of God, who does not forsake His creatures.

He had faith and lived on what he was given or what he found at hand. Never had he lacked at night a handful of straw on which to lay his head, nor had he been utterly famished. The Lord, on sending him into the lake region, had placed within his reach all the requirements of life, that he might be the model of a true believer.

Tonet mocked at Sangonera. Since he was so pure, why then did he get drunk? Did God order him to go from tavern to tavern, afterward crawling over the banks almost on all fours, with the staggering gait of the drunkard? . . . But the vagabond did not lose his solemn dignity. His drunkenness did nobody any harm, and wine was a sacred thing: not for nothing did it serve in the daily sacrifice to the deity. The world was beautiful, but when seen through a glass of wine it appeared more smiling than ever, of more brilliant hue, and its powerful Creator was admired more fervently than ever.

Each one has his own amusements. He found no greater pleasure than to contemplate the beauty of the Albufera. Others worshipped money, while he sometimes wept at the beauty of a sunset, as its fires were scattered by the dampness of the air, during that hour of dusk which was, on the lake, more mysterious and beautiful than inland. The beauty of the landscape entered his very soul, and if he contemplated it through several glasses of wine, he sighed with all the tenderness of a little boy. He repeated it: each one has his own amusements. Cañamèl, for example, delighted in heaping up golden coins: he, in contemplating the lake of Albufera with such rapture that his head hummed with verses prettier far than the ones they sang in the taverns, and he was convinced that, if he were like those city gentlemen who write for the papers, he would be able to say some mighty fine things in his drunken moments.

After a long silence Sangonera, spurred on by his very loquacity, raised objections to his own arguments, only to refute them at once. It might be said to him, as a certain vicar of Palmar once had objected, that man was condemned to earn his bread in the sweat of his brow, as a result of his first sin: but it was for this very reason that Jesus had come upon earth, to redeem him from the first fault, returning mankind to its Paradisiacal life, free of all labor. But ay! The sinners, goaded on by pride, had not heeded his words: each wished greater comfort than the others; there were poor and rich, instead of all being men: those who paid no attention to the Lord worked hard, very hard, but Humanity was unhappy, and made for itself hell upon earth. Let them try to tell him that if folks didn't work they'd have a hard time of it! Very well; there would be less in the world, but those who remained would be happy and carefree, subsisting on the inexhaustible grace of God. . . . . And this was perforce so: the world would never be a place of equality. Jesus would have to come back, to redirect men upon the right path. He had often dreamt of it, and on certain occasions when he was ill with swamp fever and when the chills attacked him, stretched out on a bank or crouching in a corner of his ramshackle cabin, he could see His tunic, purple, tightly gathered, rigid, and he would stretch out his arms to touch it and be at once cured.

Sangonera revealed an abiding faith when he spoke of this return to the earth. He would not appear in the large cities that were dominated by the vice of wealth. The other time He had not come to that vast city called Rome, but had preached in little places no larger than Palmar, and his companions were men of the pole and the net, of the sort that gathered in Cañamèl's house. That lake upon whose waters Jesus had walked, to the amazement of his apostles, certainly was no greater in extent nor any more beautiful than the lake of Albufera. There among them would the Lord come when He should return to the world to finish His work; He would seek out the simple hearts, clean of all covetousness; he, Sangonera,

would be one of the Lord's own. And the tramp, with an
exaltation compounded of both drunkenness and his own
strange belief, would draw himself erect and gaze at the
horizon; on the edge of the canal, where the last rays of
the sun were falling, he imagined he saw the slender
figure of the Desired One, like a purple line, advancing
without moving His legs nor brushing against the plants,
with a halo of light that would shine around His gently
curling golden locks.

Tonet no longer heard him. From the road to Catarroja came the loud ringing of bells, and behind the fishermen's weighing-cabin the wrinkled cover of a van came
into view. It was his people arriving. With the powerful sight that characterized the children of the lake Sangonera recognized Neleta from a long distance, in the little
window of the vehicle. Ever since he had been thrown
out of the tavern, he would have nothing to do with
Cañamèl's wife. He took leave of Tonet and stretched
himself out anew in the barn, entertaining himself with
his fancies until the night should come.

The carriage stopped before the little harbor tavern
and Neleta stepped out. The Cubano did not conceal his
astonishment. Where was the grandfather? . . . . He
had let her make the return trip alone, with the entire
cargo of twine, which filled the van. The old fellow
wished to return home by way of Saler, so that he might
see a certain widow who sold *palangres* cheap. He would
return to Palmar at night on one of the boats that dredged
up mud from the canals.

As they glanced at each other the two were assailed by
the same thought. They were going to make the trip
alone: for the first time they were to be able to speak

with each other, far from all curious glances, amid the
deep solitude of the lake.   And both grew pale, as if in
the presence of a danger that they had a thousand times
desired, which had all at once, unexpectedly presented
itself.   Such was their emotion, that they did not hasten
their gait, as if they were dominated by a strange bash-
fulness and feared the comments of the harbor folk, who
were scarcely paying any attention to them.

The driver had finished taking all the thick bundles
of twine out of the vehicle, and, with the aid of Tonet,
was throwing them into the prow of the boat, where they
formed a yellowish heap from which came the smell of
new-spun hemp.

Neleta paid the driver.   Good health and a fine trip!
And the man, snapping his whip, drove his horse off in
the direction of Catarroja.

The two remained for an appreciable while motionless
on the mud bank, without daring to embark, as if they
were awaiting someone.

The calkers called to the Cubano.   He ought to set sail
very soon: the wind was going to die down, and if he
was going to Palmar, he would have to help the boat
along with the pole for a good while.   Neleta, visibly
perturbed, smiled to all the folk of Catarroja, who greeted
her, having seen her in her tavern.

Tonet decided to break the silence, turning to Neleta.
Since the grandfather wasn't going along, they had better set sail as soon as possible.   His voice was already
hoarse, as if his emotion were gripping his throat.

Neleta sat down in the center of the boat, at the foot
of the mast, using as a seat a heap of skeins that sunk
beneath her weight.   Tonet tended the sail, squatting be-

fore the helm, and the boat commenced to glide along, the sail fluttering against the mast with the tremors of the soft, waning breeze.

They passed slowly through the canal, seeing, by the departing light of the afternoon, the isolated cabins of the fishermen, garlanded with the nets placed out to dry upon the yard fences, and the old water-wheels, of decayed wood, around which the bats were beginning to fly. The fishermen walked along the banks, pulling laboriously at their skiffs, towing them along with their sashes tied to the end of the ropes.

"Good-bye!" they murmured, as they passed along.

"Good-bye! . . . ."

And once again, silence, accompanied by the murmuring of the boat as it cut the waters, and the monotonous croaking of the frogs. The two kept their eyes lowered, as if they feared to realize that they were alone, and as if on raising their eyes and meeting each other's glance, they would flee it on the instant.

The shores of the canal were now wider apart. The banks were lost in the water. On each side extended the large lagoons of the fields that were to be filled in. Over the smooth surface the reeds swayed in the twilight, like the crest of a submerged forest.

They were already in the lake of Albufera. They advanced somewhat farther with the dying gusts of the breeze; around them they could see only water.

The wind was no longer blowing. The lake, tranquil and unruffled, assumed a soft opal hue, reflecting the waning splendor of the sun behind the distant mountains. The sky was of violet, and was beginning to be pierced here and there in the direction of the sea by the gleaming of the first stars. Near where the water met the land the drooping, motionless sails of the boats stood out like phantoms.

Tonet lowered sail and, taking the pole, began to move the boat along with the power of his arms. The silence of the twilight was broken.

Neleta, with a sonorous laugh, stood up, wishing to help her companion. She, too, could pole a boat. Tonet must recall their childhood days together, their strenuous, mischievous games, when they would loosen the skiffs of Palmar without the knowledge of the owners and scurry along the canals, often having to flee from the pursuing fishermen. When he would get tired, she would take his place.

"*Estate queta*. . . . Be quiet," he replied, his breath cut short by his effort; and he kept on poling.

But Neleta would not be quiet. As if she were oppressed by that dangerous silence, in which their glances shunned each other as though fearing to reveal their thoughts, the young woman continued to talk vivaciously.

Far off in the distance, like a fantastic shore that they were never to reach, stood out the notched line of the Dehesa. Neleta, with incessant laughter in which there was something forced, reminded her friend of the night they had spent in the forest, and of all their fears and later their tranquil sleep; that adventure seemed to have taken place only the day before; so fresh was it in her memory.

But her companion's silence, his gaze fixed at the bottom of the boat with an anxious expression, called her attention. Then she noticed that Tonet was devouring with his eyes her small, elegant, russet shoes, which stood out against the hemp like two bright stains, and something more that the movements of the boat had brought to view. She hastened to lower her skirt and remained silent, her mouth compressed by a hard look, her eyes almost closed, while a painful wrinkle could be noted between her eyebrows. Neleta seemed to be making every effort to master herself.

They advanced slowly. It was a difficult task to cross the lake of Albufera in a loaded boat moved only by might of strength. Other little empty skiffs, containing only the man at the pole, shot by as swiftly as a shuttle, being soon lost in the growing shadows.

For almost an hour Tonet had been working the heavy pole which sometimes slipped on the compact bed of shells and at others was caught in the vegetation of the bottom, which the fishermen called the hair of the Albufera. It could easily be seen that he was not accustomed to such work. If he had been alone in the boat he would have stretched himself out in the bottom, waiting for the wind to return or for some other craft to tow him in. But Neleta's presence awoke in him a certain sense of pride, and he did not care to stop until he should fall exhausted with fatigue. He was breathing heavily as he leaned against the pole to propel the boat. Without letting go of it, he would from time to time bring his arm to his forehead and wipe off the sweat.

Neleta called to him in a soft, tender voice, in which there was something maternal.

Only her shadow could be seen upon the heap of skeins that filled the prow. She wished him to take a rest: he ought to stop for a moment; it made no difference if they should come a half hour sooner or later.

And she made him sit down beside her, suggesting that

it would be far more comfortable on the heap of hemp than at the stern.

The boat came to a stop. Tonet, recovering his strength, felt the sweet proximity of the woman, just as when he would sit beside her behind the tavern bar.

Night had fallen. There was no other light than the scattered glow of the stars, which trembled in the dark waters. The deep silence was interrupted by the mysterious noises of the stream, which was aquiver with the darting of invisible creatures. The *lubinas,* coming from the direction of the sea, were pursuing the small fishes, and the black surface shuddered with a continuous *chap-chap* of disordered flight. In a nearby *mata* the coots uttered their plaints, as if they were being slain, while the *buxqueròts* sang their endless scales.

Tonet, amid this silence peopled with noises and songs, imagined that time had not passed at all,—that he was still a youngster and was in one of the forest glades, at the side of his childhood chum. Now he felt no fear: the one thing that intimidated him was the mysterious warmth of his companion, the intoxicating perfume that seemed to emanate from her body, rising to his head like a strong liquor.

With bowed head, not daring to raise his eyes, he thrust forth an arm, placing it about Neleta's waist. Almost at the same moment he felt a soft caress, a velvety touch, a hand that glided from his head along his forehead and dried the perspiration that still bedewed it.

He lifted his glance and beheld, at a short distance, in the obscurity, a pair of eyes that shone fixedly upon him, reflecting the light of a distant star. Upon his temples he felt the titillating contact of the blond, silken tresses

that surrounded Neleta's head like a nimbus. Those
pungent perfumes with which the tavern-keeper's wife
saturated herself, seemed all at once to enter the inner-
most recesses of his being.

"Tonet, Tonet!" she murmured in a weak voice, like a
tender cry.

The same as in the Dehesa! . . . . But now they were
no longer children; that innocence which had made them
cling to each other and thus seek to gather new courage
had disappeared.

The boat remained motionless in the center of the lake,
as if it were an abandoned hulk, and not the slightest
sign of a silhouette stood out against its gunwales.

From nearby came the languorous song of some boatmen. They were poling their boats over the water that
was peopled with murmurs without any suspicion that,
only a short distance away, amid the night's calm, lulled
by the birds of the lake, Love, the sovereign of the world,
was enthroned on a few mean planks.

VI

THE day of Palmar's great festival came, the *fiesta* of the Infant Jesus.

It was in December. Across the lake of Albufera blew an icy wind that made the hands of the fishermen numb, freezing them to the pole. The men wore woolen caps pulled down over their ears, and did not remove their yellow storm-coats, which, as they walked along, swished like silken skirts. The women rarely left the cabins: all the families sat about the hearth, tranquilly dwelling in a dense, smoky atmosphere like that of an Eskimo hut.

The lake had risen. The winter rains had swollen the waters, and fields and banks were covered by a liquid cloak, mottled here and there by the submerged plants. The lake seemed vaster. The isolated cabins, which before had been on solid ground, now seemed to float on the waters, and the boats were moored at the very doors.

From the soil of Palmar, damp and muddy, there appeared to rise a raw, unbearable cold, which kept folks in their houses. The old gossips of the town could not recall so cruel a winter. The Moorish sparrows, restless and rapacious, shrunken with the cold, fell from the straw roofs with a pitiful cry like the wail of a child. The guards of the Dehesa pretended short-sightedness before the necessities of poverty, and every morning a veritable army of gamins would scatter through the forest, seeking dry wood with which to heat their cabins.

153

Cañamèl's customers grouped about the fireplace and would leave their mat-weed chairs near the fire only to go to the bar for another drink.

All Palmar seemed benumbed and drowsy. There were no people in the street, no boats upon the lake. The men went out only to gather the fish that had been caught in the nets during the night, and returned as fast as they could to the town. Their feet looked huge, wrapped in bulky woolen cloths within their esparto sandals. The bottoms of the boats were strewn with rice straw to protect against the cold. Many a day, at dawn, broad sheets of ice would be seen floating in the canal, like panes of frosted glass. Everybody had succumbed to the weather. They were the children of warmth, accustomed to seeing the lake boil and the fields exhale their fetid breath under the caress of the sun. Even the eels, as Tío Paloma announced, didn't care to lift their heads out of the mud in such awful weather. And to make matters worse every little while there was a torrential downpour of rain, darkening the lake and overflowing the smaller canals. The gray sky made the Albufera dreary. The boats that sailed along in the dense mists looked even more like coffins, their men standing motionless in the straw, bundled up to the nose in thick, ragged old clothes.

But when Christmas season came, with its *fiesta* of the Infant Jesus, Palmar seemed to come back to life, shaking off the winter torpor into which it had sunk.

They must have the same good time as usual, even if the lake were to freeze over hard enough to walk on, as one said happened in distant countries. More even than by the desire for amusement, they were impelled by the wish to annoy their rivals, the folk of the mainland, those fishermen of Catarroja, who scoffed at the Infant of Palmar, scorning his diminutive size. These infidel, conscienceless enemies even went so far as to say that the people of Palmar ducked their patron saint in the waters of the canals when the fishing wasn't good. What sacrilege! . . . . That was why the Infant Jesus punished their sinful tongues, not permitting them to enjoy the privilege of the *redolíns*.

All Palmar prepared for the celebration. The women defied the cold, crossing the lake to reach Valencia for the Christmas fair. When they returned in their husband's boats, the impatient youngsters were already waiting for them at the canal, anxious to see their presents. The cardboard horses, the tin swords, the drums and the trumpets were received with exclamations of enthusiasm by the little ones, while the women exhibited to their friends their more important purchases.

The Christmas fiesta lasted four days. On the second, the music from Catarroja arrived, and the heaviest eel of the year's catch was raffled off, the proceeds going to pay expenses. The third day was given to the celebration of the Infant Jesus, and on the day following occurred the feast of Christ; all this accompanied by masses and sermons and dances at night to the music of tabor and flageolet.

Neleta proposed this year to enjoy herself at the festivities as never before. Her happiness was complete. She seemed to live in a perpetual spring behind the tavern bar. When she supped, with Cañamèl on one side and the Cubano on the other, all three tranquil and content, in a sacred, family peace, she considered herself the happiest of women and praised the bounty of the Lord, who

permits good people to live happily. She was the richest
and prettiest woman of the town; her husband was satisfied; Tonet, submissive to her will, was falling more
and more in love with her. . . . What else could she ask
for? She told herself that the grand ladies she had seen
from a distance on her trips to Valencia could surely not
be so happy as she on that little corner of mud at the
water's edge.

Her enemies murmured; La Samaruca spied on her:
for the purpose of being alone without rousing suspicion,
she and Tonet had been forced to invent reasons for trips
to the lake towns nearby. It was Neleta who did all the
scheming in this connection, with such cleverness that the
Cubano could not help wondering whether there were
some truth to certain rumors about her previous love-af-
fairs, which probably explained her skill in such wiles.
But the tavern-keeper's wife was little worried by the
slanderous gossip. What her enemies were saying now
was the same as they had said when nothing more than
indifferent words had been exchanged between her and
Tonet. And with the certainty that nobody could prove
her delinquency, she scorned all gossip, and before the
customers in the tavern she would jest with Tonet in a
manner that scandalized Tío Paloma. Neleta pretended
that she was offended. Hadn't they been brought up together? Couldn't she like Tonet as a brother, in remem-
brance of all his mother had done for her?

Cañamèl assented, praising his wife's good nature.
What the tavern-keeper did not look upon with quite so
much approval was Tonet's conduct as a partner. That
youth had received his good fortune as if it were a lot-
tery prize; he went about having a good time, like one

who does nobody any harm and consumes only what belongs to him, without giving a thought to fishing.

The site of La Sequiòta was giving good returns. There weren't any of the fabulous catches of former days, but there were nights in which the catch came very close to a hundred *arrobas* of eels, and Cañamèl enjoyed the satisfactions of good business, haggling over prices with the city dealers, watching the scales and witnessing the loading of the large baskets. As far as that was concerned, the company was a great success, but he liked a fair deal: let each one perform his share of the work without taking advantage of the others.

He had promised his money and he had given it; the nets, the tackle and all the net-sacks, which could form a heap as large as the tavern itself, were all his. But Tonet had promised to help in the work, and it might be said that he had not caught so much as a single eel with his sinful hands.

During the first nights he had gone to the *redolí,* and, seated in the boat with a cigar stuck in his mouth, had watched his grandfather and the hired fishermen empty the huge net-sacks in the darkness, filling the bottom of the boat with eels and tenches. After these first few nights, he did not even do that much. He was not fond of dark, stormy nights, on which the waters are choppy and the best fishing is done; he wasn't fond of the work necessary to pull in the heavy, laden nets; he felt a certain revulsion to the sliminess of the eels as they slid through his hands, and preferred to remain at the tavern or to go to sleep in his cabin. Cañamèl, in order to provide him with a good example and by his own actions shame the youth out of his indolence, decided to go to the *redolí* several nights, coughing away and complaining of his pains; but the cursed lazybones, noticing this, seemed only the more determined to stay away, even getting so brazen as to say that Neleta would be afraid to remain alone in the tavern.

The truth was that Tío Paloma needed no assistance to carry the business forward: he had never worked with such enthusiasm as he had displayed on finding himself the owner of La Sequiòta; but—what the devil!—an agreement was an agreement, and it seemed to Cañamèl that the youth was robbing him of something when he beheld Tonet so content with life and so utterly detached from his business.

What luck the lubber had! Fear of losing La Sequiòta was the only thing that restrained Tío Paco. In the meantime Tonet, living in the tavern as if it were his own, fattened in the delight of having all his desires satisfied for the mere trouble of stretching out his hand to receive what he wished. He ate of the best in the house, filled his glass at every cask, both large and small, and sometimes, with a mad, sudden impulse, as if the more plainly to affirm his possession, he took the liberty of caressing Neleta behind the counter, in the presence of Cañamèl and only some four feet away from the customers, among whom were some who kept a close eye on the tavern-keeper's wife and her companion.

At times he felt a wild desire to leave Palmar, to spend a day away from the Albufera, in the city or in the lake towns, and he would plant himself before Neleta with the expression of a master.

"*Dónam un duro.* Give me a *duro.*"

"A *duro!* And what for?" The woman's green eyes,

proud and imperious, would be riveted upon his: she would draw herself up with the arrogance of the adulteress who does not wish to be deceived in turn; but on noting in the youth's glance only his wish to wander about for a while, to shake himself free of his pampered existence, Neleta smiled contentedly and gave him as much money as he asked, urging him to return soon.

Cañamèl grew indignant. All this might be tolerated if he only attended to business; but no; his interests were being jeopardized, and to make matters worse, the youth was eating up half the tavern, asking money on top of it all! His wife was too kind; that gratitude which she professed toward the Palomas for their kindness to her in her childhood, was ruining her. And with his miser's insistence upon detail he would reckon up just what Tonet ate in his establishment, and the prodigality with which he invited his friends to drink, always at the proprietor's expense. Even Sangonera, the lousy tramp that had been thrown out of the place because he soiled the seats, had now returned under the Cubano's protection, and Tonet would make him guzzle till he got dead drunk, using for this purpose the bottled liquors,—the costliest of the stock, —all for the pleasure of listening to the drivel and nonsense that the vagabond had got into his head as a result of his sacred readings.

"On some fine day he'll take possession even of my bed," said the tavern-keeper once, complaining to his Neleta. And the unhappy man could not read those inscrutable eyes; he could not see a diabolical smile in the malicious glance with which she received such a supposition.

When Tonet would weary of loafing about the tavern for days at a time, seated beside Neleta, with the expres-

sion of a pet dog awaiting the moment propitious for
caresses, he would take Cañamèl's musket and his setter
and go off to the sedge islets. Tío Paco's musket was the
best in Palmar: a rich man's weapon that Tonet looked
upon as his very own, and which rarely missed fire. The
dog was the famous Centalla, known in the entire lake
country for his remarkable scent. Not a piece of game
ever escaped him, however thick the reed grass grew. He
would dive into the water like an otter, and bring the
wounded bird up from the depths of aquatic plants.

Cañamèl asserted that there wasn't enough money in
the world to buy that dog from him; but with deep sadness he noticed that his Centella showed a greater fondness for Tonet, who took him off to the hunt every day,
than for his former master, who was swathed in kerchiefs
and cloaks close to the fire. That rascal even had taken his
dog away from him! . . . .

Tonet, filled with enthusiasm for Tío Paco's excellent
hunting accoutrements, consumed the whole supply of
cartridges kept in the tavern for hunters. Nobody in Palmar had ever hunted so much. In the narrow streams of
water of the *matas* nearest to the town Tonet's shooting
sounded continually, and Centella, warmed to the task,
splashed about the reed grass. The Cubano felt a voluptuous pleasure in this exercise, which recalled to him his adventures as a guerrillero. He would lurk in ambush, awaiting the birds with the same wily savage's precautions that
he had employed in hiding in the thickets on a man-hunt.
Centella would bring to the boat the *fòches* and the *collvèrts,* their soft necks and their plumage stained with
blood. Then would come the less common birds which
Tonet so delighted to hunt: and he looked admiringly

upon the dead forms in the bottom of the boat: the cock
of the canebrakes, with its turquoise blue plumage and its
red beak; the *agró,* or imperial heron, with its greenish
and purple hue and a panache of long, slender feathers on
its head; the *oroval,* with its tawny body and its red crop;
the *piuló* or Florentine drake, white and yellow; the *morell*
or pelucón, with its black head tinged with gold, and the
singlòt, a beautiful wading bird with a glorious green
plumage.

At night he would strut into the tavern with a conqueror's air, throwing down his heap of game, a rainbow
of feathers. There! Tío Paco had a fine collection to fill
his pot with! He presented it to him free of charge:
after all, the gun was Paco's.

And when, from time to time, he would shoot a fla-
mingo, called *bragat* by the people of Albufera, with its
long legs, its big neck, its white and pink plumage and a
certain mysterious air, like that of the Egyptian ibis,
Tonet would insist that Cañamèl should have it stuffed in
Valencia, to keep in his bedroom; an elegant decoration,
since the gentlemen from the city were so eager to get one.

The tavern-keeper received these gifts with grunts that
revealed his very relative satisfaction. When would the
fellow let his gun have a rest? Didn't he find the reed-
grass lands cold? Since he was so strong, why did he not
help his grandfather nights in the work at the *redolí?*
But the rogue received the sickly proprietor's complaints
laughingly, and would turn to the counter.

"Neleta, a glass. . . ."

He had certainly earned it, passing the whole day
among the marshes, his hands frozen to the musket, all
for the sake of bringing home that heap of game. And

yet they said he fled work! . . . . In an excess of joyous immodesty he caressed Neleta's cheeks above the counter, ignoring the presence of customers and exhibiting no fear of her husband. Were they not like brother and sister, and hadn't they played together when they were children? . . . .

Tío Tòni knew nothing about his son's doings, nor did he care to know. He got up before dawn and did not return until nightfall. In the solitude of the submerged fields he ate, with La Borda, some sardines and a piece of corn-cake. His struggle to create new land kept him in poverty, permitting him no better food than this. When, after night had fallen, they returned to the cabin, he would lay down upon his bed with aching bones, sinking into the torpor of exhaustion, but his thoughts would follow him in his sleep, and he would calculate, amidst the clouds of his dreams, how many boatloads of earth were needed for his fields, and the sum of money he would have to pay to his creditors before he could consider himself the owner of the rice fields that he had created with his own sweat, palm by palm. Tío Paloma spent most of the nights away from the cabin, fishing in La Sequiòta. Tonet did not eat with the family, and only in the small hours of the night, after Cañamèl's tavern had been closed, would he kick impatiently at the door, awakening poor La Borda, who was sleepy and all tired out, to open it for him.

Thus the time passed by, until the festival season came to Palmar.

On the eve of the fiesta of the Infant Jesus, during the afternoon, almost the entire town thronged the space between the canal bank and rear door of Cañamèl's tavern. The musicians from Catarroja were expected,—the chief attraction of the festivities—and the people, who during the year heard no other instruments than the barber's guitar and Tonet's accordeon, quivered with anticipation at thoughts of the blaring brasses and the booming of the bass-drum between the rows of cabins. None felt the rigors of the weather. The women, in order to display their new clothes, had laid aside their woolen shawls and showed their bare arms, made bluish by the cold. The men wore new sashes and red or black caps which still revealed the creases of the shop. Taking advantage of their wives' conversations, they ran off to the tavern, where the breath of the drinkers and the smoke of the cigars formed a dense atmosphere that reeked of coarse wool and dirty sandals. They spoke at the top of their voices about the music from Catarroja, asserting that it was the best in the world. The fishermen from that place were a bad set, but it must be admitted that their musicians provided better music than even the King ever heard. The poor lake dwellers must have some good qualities. And noticing that the canal bank was crowded with people whose shouts announced the approaching musicians, all the customers rushed forth in a flock and the tavern was left empty.

Above the tops of the reeds could be seen the end of a large sail. As the barge bringing the musicians appeared around a bend of the canal the crowd burst forth into a roar, as if it had been inspired by the sight of the red trousers, and of the white plumes that floated above their great helmets.

The younger folk of the town, following the traditional custom, struggled to get possession of the bass-drum. The boys plunged into the waters of the icy canal, sinking

up to their waists with a daring that made the teeth of
the watchers on the bank chatter.

The old women protested:

"Condenats! .... Pillaréu una pulmonia! You'll catch
your death of cold!"

But the boys kept rushing on to the boat, clambered up
over the gunwale, amid the laughter of the musicians,
fighting for the enormous instrument. "Give it to me!
To me! ...." Until one of the boldest, tired of asking,
seized it with such a grasp that the big drum almost fell
into the water, and placing it upon his shoulder, he waded
out of the canal, followed by his envious companions.

The musicians, after disembarking, formed in front of
Cañamèl's house. They took their instruments out of
their cases, tuned them, while the dense crowd followed
their every movement with a certain silent veneration, enjoying with deep admiration this event that was waited
for the whole year round.

As they burst into a noisy march, the audience was
seized with astonishment and the strangest of feelings.
Their ears, accustomed to the deep silence of the lake,
were fairly pained by the roar of the instruments, which
made the walls of the mud houses tremble. But after recovering from this first shock that disturbed the convent-
ual calm of the town, the people began to smile gently,
titillated by the music, which came to them like a voice
from a remote world, like the majesty of a mysterious
life that was lived far beyond the waters of the Albufera.

The women were deeply touched, without knowing
why, and felt like crying; the men, straightening out their
bent, boatmen's shoulders, marched with martial step be-

flageolet and the tabor and surrounded by the jumping, shouting gamins. The women ran to get a close view of the huge fish, to touch it with religious admiration, as if it were a mysterious divinity of the lake, and Sangonera repelled them gravely. *"Fòra, fòra! . . . .* Get away! Keep away!" They would spoil it with all that handling!

But when they had reached Cañamèl's tavern, he decided that he had enjoyed popular admiration long enough. His arms hurt, softened by indolent life; he made up his mind that the eel was not for him, and handing it over to the urchins about him, entered the tavern, letting the raffle continue without him, as they carried off the beautiful creature at the head of the procession, like a trophy of victory.

There were very few customers in the tavern. Behind the counter was Neleta, with her husband and the Cubano, discussing the celebration of the following day. The entertainment committee was, according to custom, composed of those who had won the best sites in the annual drawing of *redolíns,* and the chief positions went to Tonet and his partner. They had gone to the city and had black suits made, in which to listen to mass from the first pew, and they were engrossed in going over the preparations of the festivities.

On the following day there arrived on the mail-boat the musicians and choristers and a priest celebrated for his eloquence, who would preach a sermon on the Infant Jesus, incidentally lauding the simplicity and the virtues of the fishermen of Albufera.

A barge was moored off the beach of the Dehesa, taking on a cargo of myrtle with which to cover the square; and in a corner of the tavern the fire-works maker had several baskets full of *masclets,*—little iron petards that went off like cannon.

On the next morning the lake quivered with the discharge of the *masclets,* as if a battle were being fought in Palmar. Then the canal was thronged with people, who ate their breakfasts between slices of bread. They were waiting for the musicians who were coming from Valencia, and there was much comment on the liberality of the persons in charge. Tío Paloma's grandson certainly knew how to do things! No wonder,—with all of Cañamèl's money within reach!

The mail-boat arrived, and the first to land was the preacher,—a stout priest with imposing forehead, carrying a large bag of red damask, which contained his vestments. Sangonera, out of old habit acquired during his service as sacristan, hastened to take charge of the luggage, throwing it over his shoulder. Then followed the members of the choir, who jumped to the ground from the boat: the choristers with their gluttonous faces and their curly hair, the musicians carrying their violins and flutes wrapped in green cloth under their arms, and the solo singers, yellowish youths with sunken eyes and expressions of precocious malice. They were all speaking of the famous *all y pebre* made in Palmar, as if they had made the trip for the sole purpose of eating.

The crowd let them enter the town without stirring from the bank. They wished to see at close range those mysterious instruments that were deposited near the mast, and which some porters were beginning to carry away. The kettle-drums, as they were brought ashore, caused astonishment, and there arose a general discussion as to the purpose served by these huge pots, which looked so much like the ones they used for cooking fish. The bass-viols were greeted with an ovation, and the people ran to the church, following the men who were carrying these "giant guitars."

Mass began at ten. The square and the church were perfumed by sweet-smelling shrubs from the Dehesa. The mud had disappeared under a thick layer of leaves. The church was filled with blossoms and wax candles, and from the door it looked like a dark sky dotted with infinite stars.

Tonet had prepared everything in the best of style, seeing even to the music that would be sung at the celebration. None of your celebrated masses that put people to sleep. That was all very well for the city people, who were used to operas. In Palmar they wanted the mass by Mercadante, as in all the Valencian towns.

During the celebration the women were deeply touched by the voices of the tenors who sang Neapolitan barca-rolles in honor of the Infant Jesus, while the men's heads swayed to the rhythm of the orchestra, which was as voluptuous as that of a waltz. This livened their spirits; as Neleta said, it was far better than a theatrical performance, and it inspired the soul. And in the meantime, outside on the square the long rows of masclets were being shot off, frequently drowning out the songs of the artists and the words of the preacher.

When it was over, the crowd loitered in the square until dinner time. The band at one end of the plaza, somewhat forgotten after the splendors of the mass, started up a tune. The people felt content amid that environment of sweet-smelling greenery and the smoke of powder, and thought of the pot waiting for them at home with the best birds of Albufera.

The wretchedness of their previous life seemed now to belong to some distant world to which they would never return.

All Palmar believed that it had entered forever into happiness and abundance, and they discussed the grandiloquent phrases that the preacher had dedicated to the fisherfolk; the half-ounce that they gave him for the sermon, and the basket of money that the musicians surely must cost, the powder, the gold-fringed curtains stained with wax that adorned the portal of the church, and the band that deafened them with its martial blasts.

The groups congratulated the Cubano, who stood stiffly in his black suit, and Tío Paloma, who that day considered himself the owner of Palmar. Neleta strutted about among the women, with her costly mantilla coming down to her eyes, displaying the mother-of-pearl rosary and ivory-bound prayer-book that she had received at her wedding. Nobody gave a thought to Cañamèl, despite his pompous appearance and the thick gold chain that weighed against his paunch. It seemed that it was not his money that was paying the cost of the festivities: all the congratulations went to Tonet, as proprietor of La Sequiòta. As for these people, anyone who did not belong to the Society of Fishermen was unworthy of notice. And the tavern-keeper could feel growing within him his hatred for the Cubano, who little by little was assuming possession of all he owned.

This ill humor was with him all day long. His wife, guessing how he felt, forced herself to appear amiable during the banquet which they gave in the upper story, to the preacher and the musicians. She spoke of poor Paco's illness, which put him into a devilish mood at times, and begged all to pardon him his ugliness. In the middle of the afternoon, after the mail-boat had taken the visitors off to Valencia, the irritated Cañamèl, alone at last with his wife, poured out all his bile.

He would not endure this Cubano any longer. He could get along easily with the grandfather, for that fellow was an industrious worker, and he kept his word; but this Tonet was a lazy good-for-nothing who scoffed at his partner, living the life of a prince on his money, and merely because he had drawn a lucky number in the Society drawing. He even deprived his partner of the little satisfaction that he might derive from spending so much money on the festivities. They all expressed their thanks to the other fellow; as if Cañamèl were nobody, as if all the money for the exploitation of the *redolí* didn't come out of his pocket, and all the results of the fishing weren't due to him. The end would be that he'd throw that tramp out of the house, even if it meant the loss of the business.

Frightened by the threat Neleta intervened. She counselled calm; he must remember that it was he who had sought out Tonet. Besides, she regarded the Palomas as part of the family: they had protected her in her wretched days.

But Cañamèl, with childish obstinacy, repeated his threats. As for Tío Paloma, well and good: he would go any distance with him. But either Tonet mended his ways, or he would break with him. Everyone in his place: he didn't care to share his profits any longer with that

idler who knew only how to exploit him and his poor
grandfather. It cost him plenty to make money, and he
would stand for no abuse.

The discussion between man and wife became so heated
that Neleta wept, and that night she would not go to the
square, where the dance was regularly held.

Large wax candles that were used in church for burials
illuminated the square. *Dimòni* played on his flageolet all
the ancient Valencian contra-dances, the *cháquera vella,*
or the dance in the style of Torrente, and the girls of Palmar danced ceremoniously, hand in hand, changing
couples, as if they were courtly ladies who had disguised
themselves as fisherwomen to dance a *pavana* in the torch-
light. Then came the *ú y el dos,* a more spirited dance,
enlivened by verses, and the pairs hopped about briskly,
while a tempest of shouts and cat-calls would arise whenever some girl, whirling around like a top, showed her
stockings beneath the flowing wheel of her skirts.

Before midnight the cold broke up the festivities. The
families went off to their cabins, but the younger element remained in the square,—the merry and gallant people of the town, who spent the three days of the celebration in continuous drunkenness. They carried their guns
on their shoulders, as if in order to amuse themselves in
a small town they needed to have their weapons at hand.

The *albaes* were organized. They were to spend the
night, according to the traditional custom, in going from
door to door, singing in honor of all the young and old
women of Palmar, and to warm themselves for this task
the singers carried along a wine-skin of wine and several
bottles of brandy. Some of the musicians from Catarroja, a good-natured set, agreed to accompany Dimòni's